Writing
the
Mystery

A START-TO-FINISH GUIDE
FOR BOTH NOVICE
AND PROFESSIONAL

BY G. MIKI HAYDEN

PHILADELPHIA

ISBN 1-890768-36-7

First Printing, September 2001

Library of Congress Cataloging-in-Publication Data
Hayden, G. Miki.
    Writing the Mystery / G. Miki Hayden.
    p. cm.
    ISBN 1-890768-36-7
    1. Detective and mystery stories--Authorship. I. Title
PN3377.5D4 H39 2001
808.3'872--dc21
                                              2001024764

10 9 8 7 6 5 4 3 2 1

To Lee Lozowick, Jace Walsh Szallies, and Andrew Cohen

CONTENTS

7. ON THE WITNESS STAND

8. UNDER INTERROGATION

INDEX

FOREWARD

Publication of my first suspense novel, *Time Release,* came only after what I call the "gathering of tools" period of my fiction career. Even after 15 years as a professional journalist, I basically felt as if I were starting from scratch when I first tried my hand at fiction in the late 1980s. Pacing? Structure? Dialogue? I'd never really grappled with those concepts until I enrolled in a short-fiction class at a local university extension program. I followed that with a week at the Squaw Valley Writers Conference in 1991. I also organized and began to participate in two writing groups each month, sharing tips and techniques with others who wished to write fiction. Eventually, I met an agent who saw the potential in my idea for *Time Release* and who liked my bone-headed persistence and willingness to learn. That began a two-year education during which I reworked no less than six times the synopsis of that book, learning with each step about the conventions of the genre in which I was trying to write.

All told, it took me about four years, and one unpublished "practice" novel, to develop the skills I needed to write my first published suspense thriller. For me, there were no shortcuts. And all the while, I kept pushing myself to the computer every day to exercise what I was learning. But the good news was that I didn't have to collect all the tools again to write my second novel, or the third, or the fourth. I already had gathered those tools, and I continue to gather more as I talk to and learn from fellow writers.

Others may have different stories. Maybe they have more natural ability or learn faster. Maybe they simply go to a mountaintop, receive the message, and return to their computers to then transcribe. More likely, they chip away at it just like I did—trying, failing, learning, trying again—until the sculpture finally emerges from the stone.

This book offers writers a chance to shorten their learning curve, because G. Miki Hayden has helped them put together the tools they need.

MARTIN J. SMITH   http://www.martinjsmith.com/

Time Release (1997)

Shadow Image (1998)

Straw Men (2001)

1

Introduction
to the
Mystery

— HACKING YOUR WAY INTO A KILLER MYSTERY MARKET —

Good news. Mystery now provides a real opportunity for the publishing newcomer (surprise!). Nearly every day in one of the mystery-related digests sent to me over the Internet, I read that someone has managed to sell a first novel.

Breaking into this business is absolutely possible. However, doing so is never easy. Anyone who wants to become a serious contender in the mystery world is going to have to work like a convict on a chain gang (hard). Yet access to this arena is conceivable—and this is a uniquely opportune moment in publishing history to enter the field with a well-written book.

This is why: The condition of the book business right now happens to be lousy for today's crop of mystery writers. Mid-list authors are being dumped, and mainstream publishers crave only the "breakthrough" novel that they hope will sell to one million readers or possibly more. Good news, perhaps, for the lucky few. Bad news for most of the old-timers.

But because the big publishers are handing out multi-million dollar advances to the authors whom they feel will sell hugely, the various imprints are also looking for low-end talent who will be thrilled with contracts for a few thousand dollars. So don't go wandering around with dollar signs instead of stars in your eyes. Making it into print is highly possible (though difficult), but the final result won't place you on easy street or anywhere near. And did I mention that you have to constantly work your tail off? You will.

Writing the mystery is the start of it all and we're going

to discuss every aspect here. After that, comes the seeking of an agent to represent you—also stunningly difficult (We'll talk about that, too). Then the agent has to submit your work and a publisher has to make you an offer (Easy? NOT). As for what you do next—so much is on the published author's plate it isn't even funny—you have to promote and promote. Did I say promote? Yes, you have to. We'll talk about that, too, down the line.

But I want to go back to the positive potential of mystery writing and why I wouldn't discourage any serious writers, already published or just beginning, from giving this type of fiction their optimal shot. Mystery is a best-selling genre, in competition only with romance as a hot contender for reader support. The market is huge as thousands of devoted fans pick up two or more of these books weekly and plenty select one for summer or airplane reading, at least from time to time.

Further, mystery editors will actually glance at the work of a newcomer—even, sometimes, one who doesn't have an agent. They will buy and give a contract for series work, meaning contracts often go out for two books—or as many as three—to start. This doesn't happen every day, but the possibility, however slim, exists.

Lastly, we have been discussing only the front-rank publishers, but in today's world, more places than simply the major imprints issue mysteries. Nearly every week, I hear of a new small mystery publisher—and I write the markets column for Mystery Writers of America, so I should already know them all. I don't, because there are startups all over the place, taking over from the mainstream firms, which are consolidating and, much of the time, cutting their lists.

These small presses generally will not pay the author a lot of money, but to have a novel in print might be the dream of a lifetime for many of us—and it's the start of a career for those who have other wonderful novels up their sleeves.

Happily, the small press venue continues to grow in strength. Publishers have aligned to market their authors' works and have begun to make an impression with book-stores and readers. The small publishers want to find quality content, so your novel could be next on their release list. Again, don't expect a lot of money—ever—and maybe none until royalty time; many of the independent publishers don't give any advance, at all.

From my personal experience, too, authors can retain some rights to their mysteries and sell the book else-where—overseas and for other formats. Easy? Again, no, easy would not be the word I'd use. But selling reprint or foreign language rights is certainly possible and, yes, writ-ers do it every day.

Add to the above possibilities the almost endless prolif-eration of e-book publishers, which represent a likely opportunity for a new mystery writer. Can you make money from these electronic novels? People who have pub-lished with these places tell me that they have earned maybe a couple of hundred dollars—nothing to write home about, but better in your pocket than someone else's, especially for a book that has been shopped around and has yet to see the light of day.

Authors who can't seem to get into print elsewhere (and it's hellishly hard, as I hope I've noted) can now aim for the less strenuous, but still picky, e-book venues, resulting in a cover to show family and friends, along with a disk. E-books are promotable, too, receiving reviews, eligible for awards, and a credit to your name when you send out your next novel submission.

Electronic books are happening, although not so much for fiction yet. Currently, they are a good adjunct to the print market and a great place for informational and specialty texts. The prediction is that when the computer-savvy generation grows a little older, they'll prefer to read their fiction on an electronic book screen, too. Moreover, fiction on disk may become more attractive when other elements are added to the mix, maybe short video clips or illustrations.

Along with e-books, I would like to make a slight mention of the established trend toward audio books. The audio tape business, once dominated by the publishing giants—the Simon & Schuster's, the HarperCollins's, and so on—has, along with the print book, now taken on a new entrepreneurial lease on life. This is another developing new mystery market and one that even pays some little money in advance. Watch for this aspect of the small press business to evolve, since production costs are low compared to print on paper. Here, however, as with every type of publishing enterprise, the key is distribution—the more mass the better, and mass distribution is tough to achieve.

In fact, that's what the author must consider with any proposal for a contract. How is distribution done? If by website only, sales will be minimal. Look for a publisher that distributes by traditional means, gives traditional discounts, and that takes returns. But we can discuss all this further along, in the contract and questions sections. In the meantime, let's write that book.

WHAT'S A MYSTERY, ANYWAY?

Mystery, to begin with, is one of several genres that are defined broadly by certain singular and tangible elements. Romance, for instance, is characterized by its focus on the process of attraction and courtship between two people of opposite genders. Science fiction, on the other hand, takes as its premise the assumption of a world not in evidence in our own time/space continuum.

The traditional principle behind the mystery genre is that the story considers one or more aspects of the commission or potential commission of a crime—most often murder. As with the above genres, that's a pretty big-umbrella definition. Luckily, the publishing world has been inventive and has devised whole slews of mystery subgenres, each of which has a few signs making it somewhat recognizable and distinct from other parts of the mystery sphere.

But authors can't be contained in slots that easily, so along with subgenres, we have a whole other way of looking at variants of the mystery world. In order to fit in many more subgenres (such as the thriller or espionage novel) we sometimes, for convenience, change the word mystery to crime fiction—a much looser, broader category.

But I'd like to go back to mystery for a minute because that genre name is a pretty spacious category in itself, covering such subgenres as the following:

Cozy Equals Furry Friend

Cozies are aimed at readers who want to curl up on a rainy day and relax for a pleasant hour or two with their cats (for almost certainly there is a kitty in this type of novel).

Many of the early British mysteries would be considered cozies and if you've read an Agatha Christie, that's what you've read. Due to that great author's very strong influence, the yearly cozy writers conference, called Malice Domestic (held in Washington, D.C., in early May), has named its awards (which come in the shape of giant teapots) *Agathas*.

With a cat and a cup of tea signifying the cozy, you'd better believe that any actual violence is off the page. Murder in these whodunits means a quick glimpse at the corpse, usually someone no one minds being dead. Cozies routinely involve an amateur detective, a fact revealing that the subgenres often overlap.

Amateur detective stories frequently center around a series detective who, as she or he goes about any daily business, repeatedly stumbles over dead bodies, very greatly to her—or his—surprise. Doing away with the necessity of stumbling, an amateur investigator also might be well known in her neighborhood for solving crimes. Barbara Block's pet shop owner, Robin Light, for instance, who digs for clues that commonly involve exotic animals, sometimes gets called onto the case by kids who know and trust her expertise.

Television has featured some pretty long-running amateur detective series, too—notably *Murder She Wrote* and *Diagnosis Murder*—both cozies, if television can be categorized in the same way that novels can (why not?).

Hardboiled and Cop Stories

If the detective isn't amateur, he or she must be paid, and if he's paid, he's usually a *hardboiled* kind of private investigator, or P.I. Hardboiled is the opposite of cozy, in that you sure aren't going to find any lap cats in this kind of novel. Any cats the P.I. comes across jump off of garbage cans in the alleyway—just before he gets hit over the head. Hardboiled isn't a true-to-life depiction. The subgenre is a fantasy of life, just as the cozy is, only in the opposite direction. Hardboiled exaggerates the grim elements of our world as well as the P.I.'s macho response to the hard knocks of investigation. Hardboiled detectives get kicked around, but unlike the thin-shelled Humpty Dumpty, they usually put themselves back together again, and solve the crime in the process.

The days of the hardboiled aren't exactly over, but their popularity has diminished somewhat (sorry, guys). In its heyday, favorite hardboiled authors included Raymond Chandler and Dashiel Hammett (who wrote in the 1930s), Ross McDonald (who wrote his Lew Archer series in the 1950s), Florida-based John D. McDonald (who penned series character Travis McGee in the 1970s), and Boston-inspired Robert Parker, whose long-running character, Spenser, was even made into a television series. Parker still writes, but has also acceded to prevailing trends and recently initiated a female protagonist series. Hardboiled isn't dead, however, so if that's what you write, hang in there. A resurgence just might be in the works.

Generally not to be confused with hardboiled—although some are hardboiled—is the *police procedural*. You can easily guess what the primary assumption of this type of mystery is. Most frequently, the main character is a policeman or woman, as in any of Ed McBain's 87th Precinct mysteries set in Isola—which stands in for New York City in the novels— or in Lynda LaPlante's Prime Suspect series, about a top British female cop, which first appeared in print but was later made by the BBC into several acclaimed television shows.

The structure of one of these books is exactly that, a prescribed format, in which a celebrated investigator with tons of integrity outwits, and, on occasion, even outruns, the perpetrator. The reader is constantly hit with a barrage of investigative terms and regulations, and will walk away from the story knowing more about police work than he or she ever imagined, if the author has done sufficient research. Someone such as author Barbara D'Amato, who writes about the Chicago P.D., has gone on a lot of ridealongs and sounds very much like a cop herself, but the idea that imagination counts more than fact has struck an occasional mystery writer. Legend has it that one *New York Times* topseller created a phrase that he attributed to the NYPD. Soon enough, the expression had joined genuine cop lingo as legitimate language; cops, after all, read popular fiction, too.

Another series of police procedurals that I especially like is by Christopher West, who is British, but who writes about a Chinese Communist policeman, Inspector Wang. The Russian Inspector Rostnikov mysteries by Stuart Kaminsky are also terrific, and Kaminsky writes an equally fascinating New York, Jewish cop. Read any of these and you will find out how the police—detectives, frequently—operate in Beijing, Moscow, or New York—pretty similarly, if truth be told.

Interestingly enough, the police procedural is most often written by those who are not law enforcers. The authors do what research they can and then they wing it. Some of the fingerprinting that goes on in these books might be a little bit out of date or a few degrees off in accuracy. So remember, if you're writing a police procedural, be as up to date as possible, and don't be careless. If anyone gets caught in a lie, that person is going to be the writer who's just starting out.

Legal, Medical, History Mystery

The legal mystery subgenre is a cherished favorite, often revolving around courtroom proceedings—such as made-into-films, *Witness for the Prosecution* (based on an Agatha Christie short story) or Barry Reed's more recent *The Verdict*. But placed inside the judge's chambers or on the streets, knowledge of the law and its accouterments are inseparable from the weaving of the legal mystery plot. For that reason, most authors of the legal mysteries are sworn-in members of the bar—the law thought to be so arcane that only the genuine article can set the particulars in print with authority.

Attorney John Grisham's best-selling lawyer novels, however, tend to be suspense in form rather than legal mysteries (although his first-written *A Time to Kill* is very courtroom based and the best-written of his books, I believe). Grisham's other novels also prominently feature, if not courtroom scenes, at least legal points that are essential to the process of the plot, such as in *The Pelican Brief*. So, in that respect, the Grisham books overlap both subgenres and can be named as either or both, as the mood strikes you.

As with police procedurals, accuracy is crucial to weaving a believable legal plot. In matters of the law, your execution ought to be as flawless as possible. If you're not—or never have been—an attorney, some serious research is definitely in order. Of course, much as with police procedurals, sometimes law is slightly invented by the writer. Don't take my word for it, ask the staff at television's long-running legal show, *Law & Order*. When attorneys excitedly call the producers for a case citation, half the time someone has to answer blankly with an "aw, heck, we made that up . . ." Proceed at your own grave risk, however. Knowledgeable readers don't like mistakes.

Legal mysteries, already on top for quite a long time, remain a hot button for the publishers—with a first-time attorney/author in my local Mystery Writers of America chapter receiving a six-figure advance on a proposal alone. That's one of those pinstriped suits to riches stories, not to be counted on as previewing the next attorney-author's future, although the event does point out that legal is very much sought after. The contract was for two books, by the way.

The *medical mystery* is a newer (though not altogether new) category of subgenre—perhaps originated by Robin Cook, M.D. (author of the spectacularly popular *Coma*). My own *By Reason of Insanity* highlights a neurotic but capable and caring psychiatrist, Dr. Dennis Astin. Medical mysteries involve some aspect of medical knowledge and the world of the medical professional, and, like police procedurals and legal mysteries, are riddled with profession-oriented terminology and information—although these should not be overdone. The keys to solving the crime can be of a scientific nature or not, but, in this subgenre, being a member of the health care team places the protagonist in the best spot to investigate the crime.

In a slightly different division of mysteries, which often overlaps several of the above, are the increasingly well-accepted and sought-after *historical mysteries*. Ancient Egypt, ancient Rome, turn of the last century New York City, and the building of the atomic bomb are all mystery settings that have appealed to contemporary readers. Real historic figures, too, are characters in many crime stories. Although most known persons stick to the background, some have been turned into the detectives themselves. The novelist Jane Austin, once referred to as Shakespeare's little sister, is now just another amateur detective seeking justice.

From Humorous to Shocking, Subject Sub-Subs

Bear in mind, while looking back over the subgenres, that most of the above books can fall into a further classification of humorous, serio-comic, serious, or even gritty. Dennis Lehane, for instance, now a best-selling series author, writes gritty; McBain pens serio-comic. Hollywood-darling Elmore Leonard tends toward the joking end of the spectrum; and Arthur Upfield, who wrote a classic and brilliant series about an Australian, part-Aborigine police detective, took a serious tone.

Even legal or medical mysteries don't have to be gritty or dark, but may wind up at the other extreme of the range as funny or at least amusing.

Subgenres, over time, have divided into *sub-subgenres* as well, with gardening, quilting, birding, cooking, and other well-received specialty mysteries nestling comfortably into the cozy lineage. Police procedurals, in turn, have come to involve additional types of law enforcement professionals, such as Jessica Speart's U.S. Fish and Wildlife Service Rachel Porter, Nevada Barr's National Park Service Ranger Anna Pigeon, or Linda Fairstein's prosecutor Alex Cooper (Fairstein considers her novels police procedurals and not legal mysteries because the special knowledge set offered is NYPD-derived and not prosecutorial).

In fact, the mystery publishers constantly seek other sub-subgenres that will attract niche groups of readers, and writers are welcome to create a class of mystery that is recognizable but vastly new. Maybe you're the author who has spent a lot of time game fishing or in the prevention of financial finagling and can strike out in a very different and exceedingly fascinating line of mystery exploration.

And the Category Is?

Although I have mentioned the thriller and suspense novels in passing, I want to go into the forms that don't quite fit under the general title "mystery" in a little further depth. Some authors have said to me, "I don't write mysteries," when, to my mind, they clearly do. Okay, call it *crime fiction* then.

Just as Seymour Shubin's Edgar Best-Mystery nominee *The Captain* (now back in print) clearly revealed the killer on page three—with Shubin continuing to leave no mystery as to who had done the deed—so, too, other popular writers willingly fly in the face of mystery convention. Dirk Wyle in his *Biotechnology Is Murder* forgets to put the crime into the book until about one-third of the way through. Some mystery academics would refuse to call the novel a mystery, but it is.

An editor from *Publishers Weekly* commented to me that it's a mystery to this prime publishing-industry magazine why some books are categorized as mystery and some are tucked directly into general fiction. Of course, in most cases, the choice is the publisher's, and the stores shelve offerings according to that little notification on the back upper left-hand corner of the book: Fiction goes with general fiction and mystery goes with mystery. The book dealers can't read each of the titles or ponder the subtleties before placing the volumes in the proper browsing area.

Publishers choose the category according to a perception of where the book will sell the most copies. Nelson DeMille's *The General's Daughter*, for instance, very distinctly a police procedural mystery, sits next to his other works—mostly thrillers—in general fiction. Well, certainly, because that's where the public will look for the book—not in mystery.

One category that we've only touched upon is *suspense*. Does Mary Higgins Clark write suspense, or does she scribe mystery? (She was MWA's choice as Grandmaster in 2000.) Her subgenre of suspense—or whatever slice of the crime fiction pie this is—falls into two or three divisions of its own (at least). One part constitutes what's called "fem in jep"— women in jeopardy. Fem in jep was for a while a television movie staple, but is now not quite so popular, since we don't like seeing women as weak or as victims anymore. The essential element of suspense is mounting edge-of-the-seat tension, created by having a sympathetic protagonist hurtle towards the unknown.

Another grouping under the suspense title is *romantic suspense*, some of which used to be known as Gothic romance. In these, often, the heroine is under a dark threat, but don't worry, she's clever and handling it well. On the other hand, there's a strong love interest and to her puzzlement, she can't decide if that attractive man is the source of the danger or her salvation. Nor can the reader figure it out, although hopefully our hearts will lead us to the truth. Of course, watch out—the author (you?) is going to trick us and make us sure that an evil man is good while the ultimate protector might be found holding the bloody knife.

Pure suspense, on the other hand, might have nothing at all to do with sexual politics. The dark conundrum arises from some other source. Seymour Shubin's Fury's Children begins with a killing and the reader knows who and why without much ado. The question that worries us, and that keeps us in disturbed agony until the end, is whether the good, decent journalist who tracks the young villains will be tortured and put to death by them. The stakes are high and the uncertainty is enormous.

As for thrillers, that slender but hugely profitable category, these are considered general fiction but most can also fall into the crime fiction category. These may or may not have a whodunit at their heart, but either way, they keep danger in the foreground all the way through—the more threatening, the better. Compared to the suspense novel, here the threat is much larger than the potential loss of an individual human life, with antagonists who kill serially or who threaten mass murder. Thrillers that make the readers' palms sweat and stomachs churn receive the biggest advances in the genre categories—name author or not. These are the books that have the potential for megablockbuster status. If you can write one, however, you're a more skilled author than 99.99 percent of us in print. Maybe that's why a thriller that works can be so lucrative.

Not all thrillers, actually, can be classified as crime fiction. Michael Crichton's Jurassic Park, which had readers feeling dinosaur breath down their backs, was a bestseller block-busting smash, but not crime fiction at all. Moreover, many traditional mysteries are lumped into the thriller category due to the largeness of their themes—or even their length. Lisa See's Flower Net, an Edgar nominee and a police proce-dural in form, at 465 pages for the paperback and including worldwide derring-do, was granted thriller status by her publisher and by the reviewers as well. Gorky Park by Michael Cruz Smith, another police procedural with brilliant sweeping implications and international events, was also considered a thriller.

Lastly, although the category is not last by any means, comes the novel based on true events. Tremendously publicized murders that seize the public's imagination are frequently the basis for these re-interpretations of crimes. Compulsion by Myer Levin, based on the Leopold and Loeb thrill-murder of little Bobby Franks, might be the originator of this crime subgenre, but other books spring to mind. Consider the many novels that have flowed from the killings of such victims as Lizzie Borden's parents (did she or didn't she?) and JonBenet Ramsey, or well-known killers or alleged murderers such as Jack the Ripper or Dr. Sam Shepherd.

Where in the genre will your work fall—and does it matter? Obviously, there is a tremendous proliferation of forms and you can create or expand upon one that already exists. But there are specific rules for making most of the subgenres work.

Some of the decisions that you make in your writing will be according to subgenre models. How to handle many of the elements of the novel will depend on where in the mystery world your work will fit best. You honestly should not try to sell a book that is 90 percent cozy when the other 10 percent is destined to offend that group of fans. You have to know what the audience is for your particular book and write consciously for those readers. Moreover, you will want to study what successful authors in your subgenre have already done and see which examples you desire to follow—and which not.

You can be your own creative person, but you have to understand the whats and wherefores of writing and publishing. This thorough knowledge of the mystery form will allow you to innovate wisely, rather than wildly.

———————— THE CHINESE LAW OF SECRECY ————————

I don't know why they call this principle the Chinese Law of Secrecy, but that's the name I was taught for this essential element in writing a mystery novel, pursuing a career path as a writer, or trying to get some other cherished project off the ground. The law is not a terribly complex one and runs as follows: *Keep your mouth shut as tight as possible.* For some of us, like me, that's asking a lot. I'm a blabbermouth, I like to tell the ins and outs of everything, as you might have already begun to suspect.

But the Chinese Law of Secrecy demands that in regard to plots, characters, and the hopes we cherish for our work, we keep all the blah, blah, blah, and so on and so forth, totally concealed.

Why? Because anything you leak can become less strong for you. The energy with which you reveal your plot to a friend drains from your work when you sit down to write your story. You've already expressed what you had cooking on your own personal, interior stove and now the juice is gone, or at least some of it.

Moreover, in spilling the beans (to pursue this food metaphor) you open yourself up to your confidant's negativity. "Oh, gee, no one is interested in that type of thing." "I saw that plot on *Murder She Wrote* last week." "Honey, that idea sucks." Those are the types of phrases you run the risk of eliciting.

Therefore, *Writing the Mystery* does not promote psychotherapeutic healing techniques by encouraging you to open yourself and trust your friends and mate. No way. I'm advising you as an artist to keep your work a secret, hidden inside yourself or on the page—until the work is done.

Furthermore, friends and loved ones aren't always the best critics for a work in progress. A more objective critique might be given by a writing teacher, or a writing group, but even then you need to be careful. Ultimately, there is no such thing as utter objectivity, and, besides, your work should have the opportunity to grow on its own, especially in the beginning stages.

And even when the novel is complete, please be cautious. Never tell your fellow strivers of any grand success until the ink is totally dry on the contract. The negative vibes that others might release as a result of your impassioned excitement will not be worth the ego charge of boasting.

When the book is in print, however, all secrets will finally have to be revealed—as frequently and as loudly as possible, and that's called promotion. We'll discuss that at a later time.

But while the novel is still on the stove, keep a lid on.

2

The Plot's the Thing

— To Outline or Not to Outline? (A Good Question) —

Before sitting down to write, should you develop the plot in full by way of a pre-summary or an outline? Some highly successful writers say yes and some say no. Certainly the choice is yours and what works for you depends on personality and creative factors. I don't do it, but I suggest that if you're having trouble with plotting your novel, you should try outlining, either in broad strokes or in a way that determines what will happen within each scene. That might be the trick that takes you to the next level of writing this mystery. After all, a mystery plot is intricate—you do not want to fall into contradictions that make your proceedings less believable, so pausing to focus on each action before writing might be helpful. Also, outlining can help you better visualize causal relationships between characters and events (causal relationships provoke a chain of events that will ultimately build to the climax of your story).

On the other hand, those of us who don't plot leave a great deal to inspiration—although that is going to occur anyway, with any writing task. Nothing can be so pleasing to the writer, however, as creating a composition step by step sans structural setup and watching one action flow from the last.

Here's how the *ad hoc* plotting occurs:

A character, Jennie, has red hair and, searching for a way to hide her identity (should you have her wear a hat? maybe the season of the novel is winter then?), you realize that you don't have to hide her identity at all. Instead, you create another character with red hair and a similar build.

The witness mistakes this other woman for Jennie and the other woman, you realize, is then accused of the crime. This places Jennie in a position of having to make an ethical choice and possibly admit where she's been that night—which she doesn't want disclosed for entirely different reasons. Now, in addition to successfully figuring out how you can keep Jennie's identity hidden from the police, you've created a secondary thread with the story of Jennie's alter ego.

Certainly, all the above can be accomplished with an outline, too, and by concentrating exclusively on the plot. Those who work without a preliminary scheme, however, are prone to believe that this outlinelessness (whew) permits more little illuminations and delightful twists than working with a fully pre-calculated plot could ever spin off.

But authors who plan carefully counter with the observation that prior detailing takes the uncertainty out of the mystery's direction and allows for clues to be dropped in where they will do the most good. Which faction is correct in its approach is for you to discover in your own writing.

A Decent Proposal

Sometimes, if they think they can get away with it, authors will write a proposal and send that around, instead of first completing the novel itself. In that situation, the outline must be turned into summary form, as if the novel had already been written. Presenting the book as a proposal can save wear and tear on the writing muscles, in case the premise of the novel flops. If you think that after receiving a request for the whole manuscript, you could put the book together in two or three weeks, I wouldn't entirely discourage you from pitching novels with a few chapters, a summary, and a prayer.

Mystery editors, for the most part, however, want to

know that the entire novel is available to be read. Writing a complete mystery is excellent practice, too, and gives you something to show without sweating over producing a worthwhile manuscript later, under pressure.

Those who wind up with agents, moreover, will rarely be encouraged in this shortcut approach, as agents generally present a completed mystery to the editors. Agents know that 99.9 percent of first- and even second-time authors do NOT sell on a proposal alone. The agent also likes to see the complete work to know what he or she is passing along.

Bear in mind that those writing romantic suspense are writing in the romance genre, which operates under a different set of rules. These authors are less likely to need agents to pitch a novel and will, for the most part, try to sell a story based on a partial of three or so chapters. This may be a practical necessity in that requirements for elements—from length, to type of story—vary so much from romance imprint to imprint that writing a complete novel for one or two potential markets might be impractical.

Again, the problem arises when the editor asks to see the remainder of the novel. Luckily, in the romance field, the editors are used to waiting a while for the entire manuscript. In the meantime, they have plenty other work to concentrate their efforts on—no, they won't forget that they've asked for a book, although you should enclose a copy of the original requesting letter when you send your full submission.

Chapter Length

Let me add at this point that before starting your book, you will want to decide how long your chapters will be. Approximately equal-length chapters are usually the best idea, unless you have reasons for blocking out chapters that go on longer or are shorter—and I mean good, creative reasons, not just that you couldn't stop writing or you had nothing to say.

You'll notice in looking at the books of other authors—and I recommend that you do have a peek—that some use very short chapters, while others measure off quite long pieces of text. Suit your chapter length to your type of novel. If you're writing a fast-moving cozy, the chapters can be brief with many climaxes. (Oh yes, there are climaxes at the chapter ends, or ought to be.) If you have a courtroom drama or some such, the chapters might be more extended to detail a few of the intricacies.

You will find after a while that you can feel exactly how long the chapters will be and that they divide into a certain number of scenes. Just FYI, most recently my chapters have run about 2,000 words, with three to four scenes per chapter. How do I juggle making it all fall into place so exactly? I don't. Writing to length becomes an instinctual act, over time, as does much else in mystery writing. It's like finding your way to Carnegie Hall: Practice, practice, practice.

Exercises:

GIVE IT A TRY: Start off with an outline that shows some broad strokes. Go back and break down one of the chapters. Then sketch in one of the scenes in outline form. Now try writing from the outline. Does that help? Maybe outlining is your cup of tea.

PLAN THE NOVEL: Do you know your genre? Subgenre? Think your project through. Look at a similar mystery or thriller you have at home or go to the bookstore. See how the chapters are laid out and the length of the book. Project how many chapters you will need and how many scenes. Coordinate that with any outline you write.

─────────── THE STARTER'S PISTOL ───────────

For any novel, the plot is important. The reader continues with the book because she wants to know what happens next. How doubly, triply, essential for the mystery plot to not only hold the attention of the reader, but to hold true. Many of the fans (or editors) who will pick up your story have a great sophistication about plot. Once someone has read a few hundred mysteries, only a rare one contains any surprises. Make your mystery a novel that will not only rivet, but that will keep a twist or three up its proverbial sleeve.

As we have discussed, all types of mysteries exist. Some reveal the killer in the very first sentence. But thereafter, any sort of book, even this kind, has to offer a lot for the enthralled guest (reader) to uncover. Mystery writers use devices, tricks of the trade, if you like, that can be learned and employed in driving a plot. In fact, I know a woman who worked for John Grisham's first agent. Apparently, Grisham's early work contained a lot to admire, but, nonetheless, lacked tension enough to assure the manuscript sale. Someone in the firm (title reference intended) analyzed Grisham's plot and pointed out devices that could heighten the suspense. Did that work? All I can say is—I stayed up all night reading Grisham's first published novel, a book that resulted in an unbelievable career.

What were the plot hooks that Grisham used and that

other mystery authors commonly employ? I can point to a few of them, but bear in mind that, as with every other facet in becoming a writer, much of what you personally implement in your work has to be self-taught. For now, we can latch on to some imitation.

The Opening

Why was Grisham's novel such a page-turner? One of the most compelling aspects of The Firm was the sense that something big was happening here, something that the protagonist could not control. The very start of the book exudes largeness. The new hireling attorney achieves an opulent lifestyle almost without effort, but something ominous lurks beneath the surface. Though we have no idea of what that evil is, recent deaths among the employees foreshadow great danger.

Here then is one obvious way to gain reader attention and start your mystery novel: Create a background/setting that arrests attention—and, at the same time, point out a pitfall in the depths.

Be aware that mystery/suspense/crime novels today start quickly, without a lot of time allowed for development. Editors demand this and readers are used to it. Your opening scene might be all that the editor ever sees—if you don't immediately set the tone for the book. That simply is the market today, so be aware of this factor.

One of the most-skilled authors around in regard to the opening sequence is Nelson DeMille. His beginnings can leave the reader almost breathless. See his thrillers Cathedral and The Charm School, if you want to know how to begin a novel with a bang.

I'll relent slightly in insisting that you open your mystery with a KABOOM (like the car bomb in Grisham's *The Pelican Brief*). You don't always have to begin with external action, if action isn't really your particular style. The novel can start with an internal dilemma. Even Grisham's hero in *The Firm* is really only on a search for the perfect job—not a very exciting quest, perhaps, but the venture is strongly driven by his fierce ambition.

In another mystery (such as yours) that internal combustion starting the novel can be a relationship conflict that's dynamic and sure to lead to either murder or love. You be the one to think of the dramatic hook to initialize the story, but never forget the reader standing in the bookstore staring at your first page, or the editor with several hundred (no joke) manuscripts on her desk. Your hook should hold the promise of great conflict to come.

What are you doing to open your mystery that will grab us on page one?

Exercises:

START 'ER UP: Don't just think of one way to start your novel—outline several different scenes that will be a galloping beginning to the book you plan to write.

LURE US IN: Along with the scenes, write down the elements you can add that make this opener of heightened interest—characters with money, characters with a desperate need for cash, characters with a glamorous profession, ordinary characters with whom we can identify. Set opposite characters against each other to achieve friction and conflict. Start a list and keep a list. If you don't use these ideas now, put them in your next project.

THE INVESTIGATION FOLLOWS

We've thought a little bit about the beginning of your mystery, but let's take a look at the plot, overall. Writers talk about a story arc, and that's more or less what the plotline is. Picture a bell curve, which rises gradually to an exclamation and then, topping out, descends. Flatten the apex of the curve a little bit and think of that as a few chapters (depending on your chapter length), understanding that the highpoint, or crisis, lasts for a while and then falls inevitably toward some resolution.

Speaking of arcs, keep in mind, too, that there are many mini-arcs and mini-climaxes within the novel. (I mentioned before, as one example, that a mini-climax often occurs at the end of a chapter, giving a cliffhanger effect and impelling the reader to continue forward in order to find out just what happens next.)

Have you observed nature enough to see that this type of structure exists organically? Let's look at a mountain, as one instance, which, in overview, has a structure of a peak, rocky inclines, and a valley. Within that larger configuration of the mountain, we also see intermediate peaks, inclines, and valleys—on a much smaller scale.

Or, take a look at the ocean waves hurling themselves onto the shore. Large unified surges may be spotted, but in front of these as well as behind, ripples imitate the main swell's motion. Both of these forms are models of what should happen with your plot—*one grand scheme of progression and resolution, alongside many smaller pieces with the same pattern or rhythm, which ultimately fit into and reflect the whole.*

In Search of the McGuffin

Although we've started the mystery/crime novel with a bang, we haven't talked about the *throughline* that must string the story together. That throughline is the focus of your entire novel and can be stated in one or two sentences. For example: The King is murdered during his Coronation and the Earl must find the assassin and bring down the rebels.

The motor behind the story, creating the dynamic tension to drive the throughline forward, is the conflict—here, the struggle between the Earl and those who want to overthrow the Crown. While that's the major, overall conflict, the more subsidiary contention that exists along the way, the better. Perhaps the Earl has an ongoing difficulty with the Sheriff, who feels the Earl has overstepped his bounds. Perhaps, too, the Queen hates the Earl because he scorned her years ago when she tried to seduce him. . . . These conflicts will keep the story going, presenting and maintaining the focus on the throughline in which the Earl aims to carry out his duties.

Every story in creation has a conflict and the mystery/crime story conveniently has a fairly obvious one—the crime itself and the search for a solution. This quest, akin to any typical hero's mission, is the protagonist's tireless effort to uncover or acquire what, in mystery, is known as the McGuffin.

Genius suspense filmmaker Alfred Hitchcock dubbed a sought-after article the McGuffin, remarking that anything will do to keep the characters moving ahead—purloined diamonds, a fleeing criminal, a missing document, a secret stolen by some spies. In the traditional mystery, the McGuffin is not simply an object, but the knowledge of who committed the murder and why.

In plotting your story, keep your protagonist's eye directly, at all times, on the McGuffin. While you can provide some side action, don't let any tangents go on for too long. The longer secondary matters drag on, the more the throughline gets bogged down and the less the plot can be said to work. Focus is very essential to maintaining the pace. Thrillers and suspense, perhaps even more than mystery, have to hold on to the tautness of the premise at every moment, but that incessant search must be ever-present in the ordinary mystery as well.

The Plot Thickens

This is not to say that subplots shouldn't be employed. They are delightful to the reader, when used adroitly. One or two subplots to a mystery are a big plus—but only when they converge with, or mirror, the main story. Subplots that don't coalesce with the essential search or flight that the McGuffin engine provides won't contribute to, or enhance your story. And, not only must these mini-excursions eventually come together with the central thread of the story, they must remain peripheral to the primary concern—they are secondary and subordinate to the main story, don't forget.

While subplots do add interest to a mystery or thriller, you shouldn't have so much going on that the reader loses track. Keep the strands of action relatively simple and more or less on an emotional level. Do not expect your readers to start drawing diagrams of who is who and their relation to the mystery. How many times have you heard someone complain that they didn't understand the plot? Don't let them say that about your book.

When I use the word 'simple,' I don't mean simple-minded, I mean uncluttered. An example of a quite complex story with threads that converge for a powerful effect is James

Elroy's dark and realistic L.A. *Confidential*. While many people could not follow the movie plot, the novel itself is much
clearer, essentially simple, and a great deal darker. L.A.
Confidential is a very deep, political, realistic, and compelling work. A novel such as this demonstrates that mystery
is, indeed, literature.

Bearing in mind that mystery has a story arc, we can now
concentrate on the development that leads to a highpoint of
some duration. The usual process of development in a mystery comes about through the discovery of facts by the protagonist. This discovery can be via conversation or through
documents and other artifacts—such as a gravestone, a pair
of glasses found in the wrong place, a missing pen. . . . These
objects all reveal information that clarify something particular about the McGuffin: where, what, or who it could be.

This series of conversations or discoveries is, perhaps dis-
appointingly, the whole of an average mystery plot. But while
plot is essential, it is also merely the mechanical skeleton
upon which you place what it is you are really talking about
as a writer. The plot is the form, and the form can deviate
from the traditional or it can simply follow along, with the
other elements shining above and beyond the bare bones.
Without the bones though, you have nothing to hang your
story on. Throughout development your protagonist is
amassing information—still puzzling over the hints of who
and why, or hot in pursuit, but at an intense level of involve-
ment with the facts and clues.

Since this period of development lasts more than half the
book, try to introduce several, but not too many, secondary
characters—one of whom will probably turn out to be the
villain. Add enough secondary characters to make the narra-

tive interesting and to provide variation for your scenes—but not enough to make the plot difficult to follow.

When stuck in plot development during this part of the writing (this advice for those of us who remain unplotted), you can always ask yourself which secondary character hasn't been heard from in a while and place that character in a scene. Untold numbers of mystery/suspense novels have as a structure a series of interviews with secondary characters, along with their unexpected revelations.

Suspense, thrillers, and some mysteries will additionally depend on threatening action. Add in a few dangers to build your mini-climaxes—a man lurking outside the protagonist's window, a click on the phone line, an arson attempt. Keep the danger coming, it never hurts! And be creative with it!

In Hot Pursuit

I'll return for a minute to the idea of conflict, which is what energizes your story. The conflict isn't the McGuffin, but the McGuffin produces the power of conflict. If arriving at the McGuffin were easy, there would be no conflict and no story. The McGuffin is what the protagonist is fixated on and what she, or he, desires almost more than life itself. Or sometimes, the McGuffin is needed for the protagonist's life to continue . . .

Many types of obstacles can block the protagonist from achieving the goal—finding the McGuffin. Obstacles, thus, keep the conflict and the dramatic forward motion of the story alive and produce mini-arcs. One classic detective author—someone like Raymond Chandler, but I don't recall—advised that, when in doubt of where to go with the plot, have a man with a gun ring the doorbell. The man with the gun is the obstacle that keeps the conflict and the search for the McGuffin alive.

The McGuffin doesn't have to be the same thing for all the characters, by the way, but seeking their McGuffins must cause at least the protagonist and one other to work at cross-purposes. One character might be trying to solve a murder—her McGuffin—and another might desperately be seeking election to political office—his McGuffin. If his winning the election is contingent upon the killer remaining free (for whatever reason) it presents an obstacle to the detective trying to close this crucial case. That's conflict—two strong motivations that clash and propel the plot forward.

The highpoint comes a little past the middle of your book—and there must be a highpoint—in which all of the facts and suspicions start falling into place. Obviously, this may lead to a false conclusion; in fact, it's too early for the real answer to emerge, but the protagonist is just so close. He is now racing towards his McGuffin. . . . There is a frenzy of excitement and action over several chapters. Depending on the type of crime fiction you are writing, this excitement might be more intellectual than a shootout, but this is still where a series of peak moments occurs. It is the highest point on the story arc.

At this juncture, your protagonist is really on to something, although the villain, whose identity we either now know or don't, may do something deceptive. Or the protagonist is fooling him/herself that he/she has solved the mystery.

The threat has been real all along, the search urgent, but this is a great time for those twists and turns that make the crime fiction ride so very exciting. The detective is chasing the person she knows to be the villain over the rocks. He's ahead of her, but she stumbles. A hand reaches out to steady her, or so she hopes is the intent. . . . Does this sound too trite? But there are several ways this scene can play out and sometimes even triteness can work to your advantage in that the familiar can be a positive (or a great place to play a trick), so long as it's stated in a fresh voice and intriguing characters flesh out the story.

The important thing to recall is that this is the standard structure and reasons exist not to stray too far from the form, which is dictated by a fairly common set of human emotions and internal human rhythms. Keep in mind the movie mogul who brought a film to the far outback and showed it one night to great acclaim. Inspired by the enthusiastic response, the following night, he brought another film—only to find himself torn limb to limb at the end of the screening. Naturally, the people of the village expected to be shown the movie they had loved so much.

For goodness sake, give the readers the book they are looking for—for art's sake, however, make it innovative. Employ your cleverness in creating twists and turns and dropping clues that point to wrong conclusions—at first. But don't violate a basic trust established within the genre that you will stick to typical genre conventions and genre rules.

Where you do change or stretch the rules to suit your purposes, know what you're up to and be certain you have the ability to pull it off . . .

| **Exercises:** |

CREATE A MCGUFFIN: How many McGuffins can you dream up? Write them down. You can probably spin an entire novel simply based on an imaginative McGuffin.

WHO'S THE MAN WITH THE GUN? Name a few provocative events that will move this plot, or any plot, along.

UNBLOCK YOURSELF: Save this exercise for when you're blocked in writing or in outlining. Go through your scene list and count the number of scenes per character. Find the character with the fewest scenes. Use that person in the next scene. Does that give you an idea for continuing?

THE KILLER UNMASKED

The plot has built to a frenzied climax—a level of high excitement that continues through to perhaps the final quarter of the book. Now comes the descent into rationality and clarity, step by step. This doesn't mean that the resolution has concluded by any means, just that the unwinding of the story has begun. To my thinking, nothing ruins a good book and disappoints readers like a conclusion that comes on suddenly in the last several pages, kills a few characters, explains a few discrepancies, and sweeps the stage clean.

That's kind of a cheat (not that this sort of finale isn't written all the time, even if it isn't right). After all, the entire novel, from page one has been heading toward the end result. The payoff for your audience is that light dawns and justice—even a morally ambiguous justice—is done. Take your time in delivering the ultimate prize.

What I'm trying to say here is: Don't wait until the last page of the book to reveal the big secret that you've been keeping from your readers—maybe even from yourself—this whole time. Tell what it is that we have wanted to know all along, which often might be the identity of the bad guy, well before the very last page. This doesn't mean the story is over. If your novel is action-oriented, you might have a terrific rush to stop the killer from taking a private plane out of the country, which involves an exciting fight on the tarmac. Or the protagonist might still have to gain evidence that will be sufficient to convict the killer in a court of law. Understand that the entire resolution phase must take some time if you've built enough of a mystery with adequate complexity all along. Further, the more *logically consistent* and based on the *entire* plot the outcome is, the more satisfying for the reader.

I use the words logically consistent because, in tying together the loose ends of the novel, real explanations of all your miscues, misunderstandings, and surprises have to be made. If the villain was out of town when the murder was committed, don't forget to explain how that was possible. Did he send someone else to check into his hotel in Cincinnati? Or did the killer re-set his victim's stopped watch at the scene? The reader might not recall all your characters' names, but he/she remembers the details that show you have not been on the ball as an author. Be sure to untangle every one of your seeming contradictions.

Again, clarifications and resolutions must be provided, but they must not come easy. The clock is still ticking; conflict should continue to drive the action to the absolute end. And at that point, like Arnold Scwartzenegger's character in *Terminator*, be sure your protagonist tells the readers and the editor, "I'll be back."

Exercises:

THE FINAL TWIST: List every visible character in the book and how he/she could be the killer. Right now, this is only an exercise, but you might find a new way to end your novel.

AFTER THE END: Don't stop at the end, but write out a few words for yourself telling what happens to each character after the last page. You might want to use some of the projection either in re-working the conclusion or as grist for the next book in the series.

— THE OLD RED HERRING AND OTHER NECESSARY TRICKS —

The term "plot devices" makes the authors' armory of techniques sound creaky and old. But even though you are using some of the same calculated strategies to arouse pity, curiosity, and fear as, say Sophocles, these contrivances can be as fresh as you yourself make them. While fresh works better if you don't place a red light flashing over the page on which the device occurs (in other words, if you don't signal it), sometimes even though the reader realizes that he/she is being manipulated, the mechanism can still do its prescribed job.

In mystery fiction, the rustiest device of all—that you cannot do without, unless you begin with the revelation of the killer—is the old Red Herring.

Why is it red and why is it a herring? It's a herring because if you have the hounds after the killer, these dogs will surely stop to sniff a fish on the path, even though the trail is the wrong one. Any true detective is sure to do the same, and so will the reader. But just in case the smell isn't enough to lead us in the wrong direction, the herring is red for visual attraction.

You need red herrings all over the place or you don't have

a mystery—you don't have forward motion. You have the solution and THE END, instead, or you have an investigator sitting on his duff all day, staring at the wall. But give the detective a red herring, just a whiff—"Pssst, Aunt Martha was in the castle even though she said she'd gone to London for the day. The butler saw her . . ." and the investigator is off and running in that direction. He'll subtly try to trick Aunt Martha into a confession or interrogate the butler, who obviously has his own motives for saying what he said. Maybe the butler did it himself, after all . . .

In addition to providing plenty of opportunity for the detective to get on with his job, the red herring leads to a mini-climax and probably a Twist. The twist is a wonderful device that stops the protagonist in his path and turns him completely around, leading him in a previously unexplored direction. The red herring misleads, but the twist provides a new way of looking at the mystery.

The confrontation with Aunt Martha (for instance) allows her to make a shocking revelation. This disclosure might itself be both a mini-climax—occuring at the end of that particular chapter—and the twist, although the two won't necessarily coincide. Aunt Martha's stunning confession (that she loved the dead man) might be something the investigator was already told, but adds new information (he was her brother), in which case, the moment is probably a mini-climax. If the declaration turns the entire story on its head, however, this is definitely a twist.

The contender for "best twists ever" that wins my vote is the NBC television show *Law & Order*. Some weeks the plots are filled with twist after twist, which come when you least expect them. I'll ruin a plot for you should you ever see this, but one episode is about a woman found in a coma caused by a Demerol injection. Poor young girl. We are all sympathetic and want to get the mean fellow who did it, until the twist that reveals—she did it herself (in order to implicate this guy in an attack on her). What the perpetrator/victim didn't know was that she was allergic to the medication and that she would wind up a vegetable.

We then find out that her self-inflicted Demoral injection was done in an effort to frame this man. But the real twist arrives when it's discovered that she wanted revenge on this guy because he killed her sister a few years ago. . . . Stay tuned—she's the one who really killed the sister! In this particular instance, if it weren't for the red herrings that led us to believe the girl was the victim and the man the perpetrator, the twist wouldn't have come to such powerful fruition.

Many tried-and-true plot devices succeed in helping to create a more compelling story. Again, try to make them subtle; don't signal that something is coming as a result of:

THE SETUP: Often, all too obvious, a setup prepares for a result later on down the line. The fact that there is only one key to the door can be a setup if announced well before the issue becomes a crucial one. The trick is to plant the seeds of the setup deep and early, so that the reader almost completely forgets about it, until the crucial moment arrives and the reader goes, "Oh yeah! Of course!"

MISTAKEN IDENTITY: Sometimes a setup signals a round of mistaken identity. "Jack, you're cold. Wear my coat." Bang. Suddenly, Jack is dead. Mistaken identity is a grand device, really, with many variations: the man who finds someone looking pretty much like him so he can disappear as 'dead' after killing his look-alike; identical twins, one good and one evil—or, are both bad in your story?—the woman who assumes someone's identity after a train wreck; or the man who comes back as someone else after a stint in jail or a tour of duty in Vietnam.

Mistaken identity can mean witness testimony that wrongly clears or condemns. It can mean insurance fraud. It can mean a crucial piece of evidence or a valuable diamond is passed to the wrong person. The possibilities are virtually endless.

THE SEEMING DEAD END: This is a nice device to bring out three-quarters of the way through the book to supply a mini-climax. Somehow the investigation is thwarted completely: The prime suspect has already been tried and acquitted of the murder; now, through a twist, we find out he is indeed the killer, but he can't be tried a second time. Or, for political reasons or infighting, the captain calls the officer off the case. He's sent to Brooklyn to walk the beat and so can't investigate in Manhattan . . . Or the PI discovers the sole witness is dead and the only evidence has been destroyed. To come so far and not be able to go any further! You don't think it's all over though, do you? Not with 45 more pages left to write.

HELP FROM WHERE IT'S LEAST EXPECTED: This is a nice, though not very important device. Using this, an author whose protagonist is at a seeming dead end may go on to win the day through the help of the Mafia, the prime suspect's son who is willing to be disloyal out of integrity, the suspect's secretary who has just discovered that the investigator is not exactly who she claims to be . . .

Help from where it's least expected can be exercised in conjunction with a twist—the prime suspect's son is really the guilty one and is hoping to pin the crime on his father.

The boss's secretary is in league with the boss and wants to trap the investigator while trying to appear to be a friend . . .

Little children can also help extricate the protagonist—as can dogs who bark to let an ally know that the investigator is unconscious inside the locked and burning building. I, personally, like to have frail old ladies, whom everyone else would write off, bravely help the protagonist.

EXPECT THE UNEXPECTED: One of my favorite authors, Michael Cruz Smith, has written a hero in his *Gorky Park* and the book's sequels who will do any weird and spontaneous thing in order to save the day. This is something I admire in suspense/adventure and I myself love to use this device. Your character has to be inventive and daring though, which is why writing this in is so much fun. He has to be willing to go where he shouldn't and take crazy risks. You can only use this device with a character who's a little unsocialized, which, in my opinion, is what an investigator ought to be. Go for it.

There's nothing new under the sun. Any clever tweaking of your story that you devise has probably been done by the many other accomplished authors who have gone before. But that is good. These ways of hooking the reader obviously work. I might list many of these "devices" that you can employ consciously or that you will employ unconsciously. *The Protagonist Under Suspicion, The Grudge Match, The Time Limit*—or *Else Armageddon*, and *The Evidence Cleverly Hidden in Frequently Trod Ground* are examples of the other countless old devices that work.

When in doubt, throw in a red herring, or a twist—turning the reader in a whole new direction. Maybe you know who the killer is—and maybe you don't. Maybe the last red herring you throw in will actually lead to the honest-to-goodness killer. . . . Make it look like a red herring and then disclose that this clue is for real. Oh yes, that is a twist that's been done before . . . (but a good one).

| Exercises: |

LIST 100 DEVICES: Okay, 100 is too many, but make a list. Think about those devices and why they work. You'll hit upon one—or more—that you'll want to incorporate in your own mystery.

SPOT THE DEVICE: Consciously look for devices in all the television shows or movies you watch. Even stories that are not mysteries use devices. Can you borrow a device from comedy to use in your mystery?

3

Accessories to the Fact

Plot vs. Character

What counts in mystery isn't simply a clever means of murdering someone. Although many short mystery stories are based on that alone—and even win awards without extensive character development—this type of presentation is actually out of favor.

At one time, mysteries tended to cleave to a strong plot. Even those written by the Golden Age of Mystery masters (Agatha Christie, Ngaio Marsh, et al.), which had strong and well-designed characters, were still dependent on their plots to arrive at a thumping good conclusion.

In the more recent period of the mystery, the plot has lessened its hold on the novel, and character has become the force controlling the book. Editors are actively seeking interesting and engaging protagonists. So-called "puzzle books," with little or no characterization, have not been very much in demand.

Exactly what is meant by characterization is rather debatable, because many of the contemporary characters driving books of character are more or less cardboard cutouts (to my eyes), but with some "trick" that works for the reader. Many of these salable characterizations have included the forceful woman PI who is superb at repartee, or a criminal protagonist who blunders into (somewhat) going straight. These characters may or may not be full and real, but they have held their own in the literary marketplace, alongside more complex individuals, who smolder or otherwise ponder their personal destiny on the pages of the most-current detective fiction.

Personally, I like character-driven novels, such as the one

I just finished reading: *Death of a Red Heroine* by Qui Xiaolong from Soho Press. At about the midpoint of the novel, the identity of the killer is pretty well established, but the quandary turns to what will become of Chief Inspector Chen. Chen is such a real character and such a decent guy, that worry was foremost on my mind as I sat up late devouring the remainder of the 480 pages. If the story had been solely a plot-driven one, I might well have peeked to see what the ending was, so that I could go to sleep. I didn't.

A strong plot is a plus, I will never argue with that fact. We all like to be surprised. But the element that magnetizes most readers to the mystery is the human one. People enjoy identifying with others of their species, their weaknesses and their strengths. If the flaws are too great, on the other hand, we want to disassociate. (The really flawed person, unless goodness lies underneath, is designated the villain.)

The reason that readers buy a dozen books in the same mystery series is arguably not because they have been surprised each time by who the killer is—even though that's a nice extra payoff. They buy series books because they have developed an attachment to the protagonist and other characters who gather around him or her.

I know I feel at home with the cops on *NYPD Blue* or the attorneys in *The Practice*. I like watching these shows because I am well acquainted with the people, although I sometimes enjoy the plots as well. I wouldn't miss an episode of either.

A number of bestselling authors, however, don't write a series—take John Grisham again, not a writers' writer, but someone who has gone where we'd all like to go—into multiple printings. Still, although each book of his has a different protagonist, all his lead characters have the same sense of basic integrity. We can rely on that, as well as the pursuit of a little excitement, sometimes from slightly silly plots.

In other words, even in a mystery starring a hardboiled detective, you have to make the reader care. Oh sure, he is an alcoholic and a womanizer, but that's because underneath, he's oh so vulnerable. Make your characters three-dimensional. Let them come across as real people with real life insecurities, faults, and personal issues.

Writing the mystery is truly a balancing act in creativity. The plot has to be finely tuned too, a fact that editors have stated to me in discussions of what they are seeking. Be sure, therefore, to deliver on the plot side as well as on the style, background, and character elements. You must keep the tension up, the action flowing, with enough twists and turns so that there is no stagnation. You can insert false leads, imagined danger, misunderstandings. But all these sidelines have to contribute to the working out of the solution.

Actually, bravo if your protagonist can "work" the solution out, as this makes a good story even more formidable. He or she is the type of investigator we truly admire. I think it's a very hard conclusion to deliver, however. The more common way a crime is solved in post-Sherlock Holmes fiction is by a key witness coming forward or the bad guy confessing or being forced out of the woodwork through some ploy. I've never seen them actually single-handedly solve a murder on NYPD Blue, have you? But I'm devoted to the show, despite the fact that their answers come from having the killer already at hand or having him/her turned over by someone else. Hey, the same is true of most cop shows I've ever seen and, in reality, that's the way the police usually do it, according to a detective speaking at one seminar I went to.

True to life doesn't mean true to fiction though and the more actual detection you can combine with stunningly fascinating characters, the better. However, such a class act isn't easy, and many top mystery writers don't accomplish it with every release—or even ever.

In the end, most mysteries only *seem* to be based on who held the knife when it plunged into Uncle Martin's chest. Mysteries really are stories that follow a person who has characteristics that we admire—especially sound analytical thinking and a mania for justice. Create someone we feel for and we'll see you through your other writing flaws.

Exercises:

WHAT DO YOU LIKE AND WHY? Professional writers must remain aware, as you see, of what underlies fiction. You have to both react and observe your reactions when you read or watch a mystery. If you liked the last re-run of *Barney Miller* (a cop's favorite), ask yourself 'why?'. Did the plot get your brain cells going? Or did you identify with the main character? You yourself are the test subject against which to measure what is most effective in fiction.

STEAL THAT PLOT: Did I say 'steal'? Surely not. I meant, if you do admire a plot, pick up a notebook and write down the salient points. You might want to 'borrow' some of the structure for your own project. Don't forget, everything has been done at least a dozen times before and will be done again—so this isn't a crime.

THE 'WHO'S' IN THE WHODUNIT

The person you probably already understand best in your story is your protagonist. You might not know what aspect of yourself that character represents and he/she might seem nothing like you, but this is someone who exemplifies some part of yourself—maybe a part you've never expressed, but would like to.

Your character might be shy and withdrawn because that's who you are, and you'd like somehow to explore and validate the shy dimension of yourself. Or your protagonist might be bold because you'd like to see what your own bold facets in action might feel like.

Even if your character is chosen to represent someone in real life—an O. J. Simpson character, perhaps—you're going to draw from yourself to build that personality. That's how actors create a character on stage or screen, narrowing in on an internal reality that most closely matches the persona given the character, and that's how you, the author, will draw your protagonist as well. This is why a large experience of life can give the writer a great deal of reality to draw upon. On the other hand, depth of imagination and a certain mental freedom to explore inner space can lead to the same type of authentic expression.

But do be sure to make your protagonist real. Just as audiences can tell when an actor is faking it, so can readers perceive a falsity on the page. The truer you paint the protagonist, direct from your emotion to the mystery, the more the reader can identify with that character. The reader will then fear for him or her and want to read more, know more, of who he/she is.

For a great many mysteries, as I have said, plot is a secondary thing. Authors may be known for formulaic plots, but people are so drawn to the protagonist that they want to get the next of that writer's novels. One good example is author Dick Francis, who, though he doesn't write a series character, has protagonists who really are all the same—as is the situation in which they find themselves, essentially. But Francis has been wildly popular. Why? His protagonist stands true and decent, self-sacrificing as we'd all like to be in a similar fix.

Our Bond with the Protagonist

I'll mention again that most main characters are completely personable. Silly and bumbling, or heroic and sure, the thread that ties these leading men and women together is likeability. If we don't feel an attraction to and admiration of them, we don't want to read on. . . . Most of the time. Then along comes a protagonist like Tom Ripley. Don't let the recent movie, The Talented Mr. Ripley, fool you—in the original Patricia Highsmith novel, Tom gets away with it. In fact, he continues to lead a life of crime—although not usually one that involves actual murder. But then, although Ripley is disreputable—to say the least—he is congenial and charismatic and we don't mind being taken along for the ride.

Permit me to put in a word of warning about creating a character who has some "issues" of the Ripley type. Be aware that many editors won't tolerate such hanky panky on the part of the protagonist. We're very politically correct these days and the hero or heroine ought not to step beyond a certain line in committing questionable acts. Curb your protagonists, ladies and gentlemen, please, if you're looking for a mainstream publisher. If, on the other hand, you're going for an independent press that might like a novel a bit more edgy, you can be somewhat more venturesome—and best of luck.

How then, do you sketch a person in words? Physical description? That's a start, but combine the physical with a consideration of how that applies for maximum effect.

He used his six-foot-four solid frame as a means of dominating the others on the team, but his real aggression was of a psychological, not muscular, type. Penetrating blue eyes shined out a warning of danger to come, should you cross him. That look dropped a potential voice against him quicker than any raising of his powerful and knotted bicep could have done.

In other words, you must draw a character *actively*. Although we are not moving anywhere in the above passage, the *effect* is active, not static, with the character under the microscope as he lives and breathes. His qualities stand in relationship with his everyday interchanges and are not simply fill-in-the-blank height, weight, and eye color.

Other Cast Members

In a mystery, secondary characters also very much count and the attitude they take on usually depends on the type of novel you have in mind. Try to stick to the truth with your secondary characters as well as your protagonists, but remember, the readers don't have to identify with them— although they do have to believe that this type of person could really exist.

We've all met people in real life who have been so over

the top, we were incredulous. Oddly enough, in fiction these folks sometimes are too jarring or unbelievable for the page. At the same time, however, you want to color your characters and make them memorable—it's a fine line to walk.

Whatever you do with characters, please, please, don't draw stick figures and expect that to work. Again, something real must shine through. Often, new writers are told to select a mannerism that will be used to describe or characterize the person being sketched. Please don't do that. Your secondary characters can be based on someone you know and drawn from life or even derived from a character in a movie you once saw. But they have to show an inner logic and not just outer tics. The closer you get to the way real people behave, even if you clothe these characters in comic dialogue or place them in an outrageously bizarre situation, the more believable your crime drama will be. Work, work, work on your secondary characters. They must be more than mere plot devices or they will be entirely uninteresting and kill the drama of the story.

How do you find and create characters? I've suggested one possibility—that you draw on a real-life example. Is there a talk show host you've observed a lot? Or someone in your workplace who could be a figure in your mystery? The good thing about using people who exist and placing them in a situation in your book is that they arouse real emotions inside of you and will elicit that in your description and dialogue. Again, this will add a dimension of genuineness, even if the person is a character in a movie you once saw, a character who made an impression on you.

Many thorough authors will first write a biography of

each important member of the cast. That's one way to go and creating the bio does seem to help some writers know those individuals who people their novels. Try sketching a few of your second-line figures, if that appeals to you. People often have a central theme. Try and identify and explain that individual's main issues. Or describe some of the people you know in this type of profile and see if it works, before basing your characters on a similar set of factors.

In my own work, I don't do that type of thing, as I don't struggle with the characters' psychology. But whichever track you take with characterization, just be sure that your people—even your most comic ones—carry a full load of ordinary human emotions, personality tics, and complexities.

Enter the Bad Guy

Of course, most mystery/crime novels will have a villain or villains and there are two approaches to writing your antagonist. A villain can be shown as someone like you and me, with either a situation that evokes the bad behavior or slight character glitch that leads to a crime. Another way of drawing the villain is as a through and through evil individual. While I suspect that out-and-out bad people—psychopaths or evil persons—actually live and breathe, I've never met one. The one killer I met (who murdered two women sequentially) was someone who was terribly confused. Yet one hears items on the news that make it seem that pure evil does, indeed, exist.

The villain is the one character, to my way of thinking, who can be less true to an inner reality we all recognize. In the person of the perpetrator, we cross over to the allegorical; the guilty party is the symbol needed to drive the entire action forward. Mystery and crime fiction are about good versus evil, after all—an exorcism in which justice and virtue hopefully triumph. To carry out this primal theme, exaggerating the depths of depravity of a villain never hurts.

Usually, the author's judgment must fall harshly upon the perpetrator because the editor awaits this particular denouement. Most editors feel that this condemnation of the killer and disassociation from him or her is what, in the end, the reader seeks—a conclusion that may, for the most part, be the actual case. We don't want to identify with the villain, and the more evil or demented he/she is, the less of ourselves we see or want to see in this person. On the other hand, crime fiction that falls into the noir subsubgenre, a gritty division of hardboiled, can offer a moral ambiguity at the end. This type of novel is a rarer sort, suited only to particular tastes.

Exercises:

WATCHING BUILDS CHARACTER: You might never use them for a piece of work, but keep your eyes on two or three people at the office or in a group to which you belong. Study what makes these folks exactly who they are. Pick someone you think interesting and someone uninteresting and see which signals tell you about their character. Don't invade their privacy or stalk them, please.

THE COMMON CRIMINAL: Because most of us don't work in prisons, or deal with criminals on a daily basis, writing a convincing bad guy can be difficult. Take a couple of accounts of crimes from the newspaper and write an analysis of the person who could have done such a thing. Hey, you might have a story there.

OFFERING TESTIMONY

Editors want to see dialogue. Interchanges between characters, terse and to the point or chatty, are the contemporary standard. Speech, speech, speech is what our society is based upon. Pick up a couple of novels and leaf through. Which pages attract your eye the most—those with solid, descriptive text, or those that include only a few lines of dialogue?

I can tell you right now that the pages with dialogue have the most appeal because they provide a resting space for the eyes. So, visually alone, dialogue is necessary in your writing. Beyond that, however, dialogue allows a change of pace and a chance for the reader's mind to relax.

Dialogue adds variation to any story and facilitates the progression of action. The actual words of a character, too, can often convey the character's mood or his intentions with much more subtlety than can description. A great deal of your characterization will be accomplished through dialogue, as that is where we hear the character's actual "voice." In short, dialogue is necessary, and the mystery author must learn how to handle it smoothly.

As with everything in the writing field, schools of thought war over the use of verbs that punctuate dialogue. Some purists insist that the word "said" is the only way the act of speaking should be described. They claim the word is invisible. That is probably true up to a point, and the word "said" is relatively neutral so that the verb can be used with some frequency and still remain in the background. Overuse "said" though and even that verb will be clanging in your readers' ears. Ouch. A good word for journalists' use, "said" is not the only past tense verb a fiction writer can employ to denote the act of speech.

In my very personal opinion, characters can mutter, murmur, accuse, beg, explain, exclaim, observe, order, triumph, agree or disagree, and much, much more without being inappropriate.

Despite a preponderance of "saids" in one of Edgar award winner Stuart Kaminsky's Russian police procedurals, his characters sigh, whisper, shout, call, ask, correct, repeat, and respond.

The men and women in Laura Lippman's Edgar-award-winning PI series urge, offer, plead, assure, and confirm—but mostly journalist Lippman does use the "said" approach, or, as is a common pattern in author Linda Fairstein's books, doesn't employ attribution at all.

Adverbs can also be used to help along the verbs describing speech, as in *he said gently, she grumbled feebly,* or *he insisted knowingly.* (Some writers, too, hate adverbs with a fury—I'm a moderate fan.)

Essentially, any of these approaches may be used, so long as the person speaking is made clear, either through the words themselves or by adding the name of the character—as in *said Holly.* The author should also aim for some variation in structure—always—when writing dialogue.

In other words, for one patch of dialogue, you might write:

"Hello," Eric called when he saw her.

"There you are," she answered in surprise. *"I looked for you on the patio."*

Let's continue their conversation. Pay attention to what feelings, or lack thereof, are conveyed . . .

"You looked for me? I'm glad you did."
"Yes. I wanted to discuss Uncle Myron's will."

Naked dialogue will do to convey facts, but the emotional communication is limited and ambiguous. So unless the feeling is of minor importance at that point, dressing the dialogue with actions may help with characterization and transmit what is happening between the characters. (Although don't forget the need to vary your formats.)

"You looked for me? I'm glad you did." He smiled seductively.
"Yes. I wanted to discuss Uncle Myron's will." Her mouth quivered and her voice broke.

Please note here that though this dialogue is all nonsense and the situation based on nothing at all, that you've suddenly become a little bit interested in these characters and the nature of their relationship. What type of man is he that he smiles at her seductively? Does he do that with every woman he meets? Does he like her? Or is he trying to annoy or intimidate the woman? And what in the world does her reaction mean? That's the power of dialogue combined with well-chosen annotations.

I might also insert a few other little tips here about your characters' speech: Make the dialogue as natural as possible, but don't reflect how people talk to one another in real life. If you listen to genuine speech even between two intelligent, educated people, you will hear a lot of awkward phrasings and stumbles that don't belong in a published novel. Therefore, don't make the dialogue so real that you feel you're actually eavesdropping, only make it "seem" quite natural—there's a difference.

Further, while your characters might each have different speaking styles, which could work effectively, don't allow those styles to appear to be poor writing. You might perceive the character as saying *you know*, a lot, but don't put it in the dialogue where it will annoy. Instead, say, *he spoke hesitantly, unsure of himself* or *his manner of speaking was unpolished,* to let us know a detail about the character without getting on our nerves as readers.

What about other languages and dialect? A little goes a long way, just as with a strong spice: Use sparingly. You can also say, *Though Roger spoke in the accents of the street, Jane seemed to hear him in the language of her class . . .*That or some other explanation can allow you to write the dialogue in plain English for the reader's ease of use.

The main point to remember is that dialogue is necessary—lots of it, pages of it. Always make clear who the speaker is. Vary your means of expression, or the repetition of form will begin to clank as loudly as a cymbal.

Exercises:

WHAT DID THEY SAY? Try to reproduce a conversation you heard recently. This might lead you to understand how written dialogue differs from actual speech. Rewrite the conversation in dramatic form.

DARE TO COMPARE: Take a few sentences of dialogue and try them unattributed, then with simple attributions, and next with action and description between the comments. What works best? Ask a critique partner for his reaction as well.

THE SCENE OF THE CRIME

Mysteries aren't set in the middle of nowhere. In fact, the more they are attached to a real time and place, the more likely they are to get some editorial attention. Editors, however, have firm but changeable opinions as to which background settings are the most likely to sell to the public, a fact that makes choosing a setting a little bit tricky. Further, not every imprint looks for the same type of setting in its books. Some publishers seek out exotic backgrounds and others forbid overseas locales.

Compounding that confusion, what the various houses look for is likely to change—probably just as you are finishing your novel. For that reason, I'd suggest not paying the utmost attention to what is being sought, but maybe keeping an eye open . . .

In general terms, most U.S. publishers don't care for settings in other countries. However, Nelson DeMille's *The Charm School* was set in Russia, the setting of most of Michael Cruz Smith's *Gorky Park* and sequels. Berkeley reprints British author Christopher West's novels, set in China. Soho Press exclusively seeks out foreign locations for its mystery line. And Intrigue Press has recently introduced WorldKrime, a unique line of mysteries that aims to bring the American reader a better understanding of various world cultures through their criminal element.

A few years ago, the mainstream mystery editors were saying that they didn't want to see any more New York City backdrops—too many authors live in New York and set their mysteries here. This probably remains fairly—but not exclusively—true. Also true is a preference for regionals—novels set in places such as Michigan or Minnesota. Then we have the subgenre of the Florida novel—Florida somehow being considered a place where strange people do strange things. (Looking at the crime rate nowadays in South Florida, that's likely so.)

My best advice in this regard is to remember just how important setting can be. A fairly specific background will impart a lot of interesting color and reality to the novel, grounding the story in a place (and time) and adding to the information and entertainment value. Which is why a setting must be well researched.

You don't have to live in Nebraska to write about it, although intimate knowledge of a spot doesn't hurt. You do have to take out some maps and go to the library or forage online to see pictures of the place and get solid information. Ask questions of someone who lives there. The more vivid you can make the setting, the more likely you are to have an entertaining mystery that will sell.

Allow me to add that I *often* write settings I have never visited. Maps are the best help in providing street names and highways, as well as natural terrain such as mountains and lakes. This description can be real enough to be believed by those living there.

However, I suggest you exercise great caution in employing an unfamiliar setting. No glitch has remained in my mind so vividly as the mystery author who placed a scene in a revolving hotel restaurant on Miami Beach, a city I have known for many years—a city without any such eatery to point to, in reality.

One last consideration: Like Ed McBain with his 87th Precinct series set in Isola, you can place your mystery in a city that you make up. I used an imaginary city myself in *By Reason of Insanity*. No fear that you will make a mistake when the city or town is your own invention.

Settings in a Smaller Sense

Settings can also include the path to your house, the room inside the house, the car, the boat, every bit of the close and intimate jungle in which your characters live.

These, too, are created by description, just as the larger, commonly acknowledged settings of New York or Miami or Pittsburgh are sketched out. This micro setting—the protagonist's house, for instance—is less likely to be based on a real model and, so, more depends on imagination. But also, you are less subject to a challenge on the results, unless they are inconsistent, droning, unclear, and so on.

The purpose of setting is to give your characters and their actions context and dimension. If your protagonist's office is messy, we know something about her personality. If a detail of the setting will add to the action—e.g., the killer escapes through the French doors—we also want to be able to visualize the piece of the scenery to which you refer. Establishing the place description ahead of time might sometimes be useful to this end.

But more than anything, having your characters exist in a carefully detailed environment grounds them in a concrete reality. Because the old oak rocker is named, the man who sits in it must also possess a solid identity.

Further, sometimes in a mystery novel, we might try to create a certain atmosphere—either a dark one, or one that is deceptively bright—a bright setting for a hideously dark deed. You must bear that in mind, too, when you create a smaller setting. What emotional and mental impact are you trying to achieve? You don't always have to correlate one for one, either, as I have just suggested. You might strive for a contrast between the environment and the action. A beautiful, formal garden on a bright sunny day might be the perfect setting for a murder. But so might a gloomy forest in the drizzle and damp.

Describe, but actively rather than passively, and draw us into the scene.

Exercises:

DAMP DOWN THE DULL: Sometimes descriptions of settings can be boring to read. Write a description of an area with which you are familiar. Go back though the same sentences and place your character there, driving or walking and thinking. What can your character do to make this setting more interesting?

BUILD THE HOUSE: Take a section of dialogue you've written and call in the decorator (you). Intersperse descriptions of the set. If Malcolm sits, make sure he sits on Jane's white leather couch. If Nancy is talking, let her open the refrigerator and check the contents, while she chats. Make sure that your characters have a setting to back up their existence.

PINNING DOWN THE DETAILS

Research: I recommend it! If you want to add specificity to your mysteries—and you do, as well as factual correctness—research is essential. Hitting the books to uncover information, to my way of thinking, is also a lot of fun and improves the author's general knowledge base, maybe just for understanding and enjoying the world.

Research is re-usable, as well. In researching the Navajo for a book not yet published, I was able to take that same information to write a couple of short stories. One, a children's short, made it into print some time ago. The other, "Shaman's Song," is in the anthology Unholy Orders: Mystery Stories with a Religious Twist, issued in 2000 by Intrigue Press.

Moreover, I used some of the same research in my short mystery "Codetalker," about the Navajo who served in the Pacific in World War II, which was published in Futures magazine.

Research can be serendipity—a happy accident. I always buy books, sometimes secondhand ones, that I think will yield a lot of juicy and interesting facts. I bought some books on Hawaii this way and thus wound up with the Hawaiian Islands as a setting in Pacific Empire and for my story "Like Stuff Happens, You Know . . ." which was published in Murderous Intent Mystery Magazine.

Maps are an excellent source of information. An Atlas is nice to have, but can be expensive. Maybe you don't want international settings, anyway. A nice set of U.S. road maps can be relatively low-cost and filled with lovely detail. I use these all the time in working on setting.

Secondhand books are terrific, too. Some information goes out of date (the particulars of the law and police procedure, for example)—but some, such as medical information, almost never does. I have an anatomy book from way back when. We still all have the same body parts (except for one muscle found actually only a few years ago somewhere in the jaw!).

History is fairly unchanging, as well. In fact, the older books covering an era in which you're specifically interested can be better than more recent books. John Toland's *The Rising Sun*, about Japan's role in World War II, contains real interviews that Toland conducted at the end of the war, and is a great source of information and attitudes. Yes, I bought one of the volumes secondhand for a few dollars.

The Cheap Author's Guide to Research

Of course, many people might not want to spend the money for "just in case" literature. That's fine as well. We all know the quantity of information that exists online is virtually endless. It's possible to find amazing bits and pieces on the Internet—the words to an old spiritual perhaps, or a poem never copyrighted. (Watch out for copyrights. You must not violate those. And the words to songs, beware, are not cheap if you want to pay for reprint permission.)

Libraries also offer a lot of value, as does your local bookstore, which can be used much in the same way as a library. Nowadays, sitting and cruising through books is perfectly acceptable and you can get hold of a greater variety of new, topical books than in the library. Even in remote hometowns, you'll usually find one good bookstore to use for research. Make a list of the facts you're seeking and go. Or if you simply want a background in a particular topic, pick a seat—or sit on the floor—and read. That's why bookstores have cafes for coffee breaks. Make a day of it.

Research is important. Facts sprinkled through your mystery can make the book more vivid and authoritative. Don't copy facts into your novel, but incorporate them skillfully and unobtrusively. You don't need to use every fact you've picked up in your outings, either. Only use a necessary piece of data and rework it later on so that "background" information remains in the background and doesn't seem to take center stage.

A unique time period or protagonist's occupation—even though you don't share it—can make a book a more attractive "buy" for the publisher. You don't have to enjoy intimate knowledge of a topic to make that subject part of your character's world and add value to a plot and characters that work.

| Exercise: |

FOR THE HECK OF IT: Begin to collect material on one or two subjects that interest you, reading a bit as you go. The next time you want to start a story, use this research. You're set.

THE STOLEN KISS

Romance is a definite plus in any mystery. While in a romantic suspense novel, the love interest outweighs the mystery element, in a mainstream mystery, the spark between two characters offers a secondary plot line and can add emotional depth to your story

Romance is not essential in a mystery, however, so don't think you must, out of necessity, add the love line. Many stories hold up without that particular device. Furthermore, the romance doesn't have to be between the protagonist and his/her opposite (as in the growth of love between the detective and his wife in *The Concubine's Tattoo* by Laura Joh Rowland), but can derive from a related thread, such as between the defendant and his wife (*Anatomy of a Murder*). Not everyone cares for a love story, either, but having one is handy, just in case a whole set of readers look for such a development after the discovery of the corpse.

A romance also offers the opportunity for a built-in conflict that can add to and help drive the plot. The behavior of the lovers, or would-be lovers, can be used to stir the action up. Passions of the heart might further add motivation for either the murder or for solving the crime.

My suggested rule of thumb for incorporating a love story into your mystery is to make the romance part and parcel of the plot, not just a sidebar that is unrelated. If the protagonist's assistant goes around moaning about his love for Emmy Lou, have Emmy Lou be the former fiancée of the deceased, now afraid to reveal too much lest she alienate her current boyfriend. He, for his part, is overwhelmed with jealousy, which interferes with his pursuit of the investigation.

Don't allow the romance to get away from you, either, going on and on. While some romantic mysteries work quite well, others have found themselves blown off track by too much l'amour, l'amour. Even when the investigator's new beloved turns out to be the killer and a conspirator in a terrible plot, that's no excuse for spending 50 pages on their otherwise irrelevant outings. Such carrying on is a distraction from the focus of the story. The love might be torrid, but make the scenes brief and at decent intervals.

Unless, that is, the story is categorized as romantic suspense. Romantic suspense meant to sell to one of the romance publishers should follow a rule exactly opposite to the one I just cited. The love affair is in the forefront in such novels. While the heroine might suspect the hero of the crime, she is irresistibly drawn to him, anyway. . . . The crime occurs within the story and the quest for the solution can't be disregarded, but the possibility that the hero and heroine might come together is truly the focus of what you are writing.

Never set the romance aside in romantic suspense and never descend to the level of the gritty or overly graphic. Crimes in romantic suspense should be offstage and more suggested than spelled out. And please—no rape. That's okay for a certain type of mystery, but an absolute no-no in romance of any type.

Exercises:

LOVE 'EM OR LEAVE 'EM: A lot of writers have problems writing love scenes—and I'm not talking about sex scenes, which are a trifle out of date. Take your main characters, or any characters you choose, and write a few paragraphs describing a romance between them. You certainly don't have to leave the love scene in the novel, but the interaction can give you an idea of how these two come together—or could. The exercise might add to the chemistry between the two as you write. Even if Joe and Lisa never become involved, that undercurrent will be there, and draw the reader.

THE ODD COUPLE: Playing your characters against type can make them more intriguing. Jot down some ideas for couples in your book who would never be viable partners of the heart. Create a generic scene and drop in your various characters. Anything strike you?

THE BLOODY DEED

Violence has to be presented with great care in any mystery. But what this means is completely subjective. Some writers are extremely popular despite—or due to (who can say?)—a level of gruelingly bizarre, sadistic material in their work. They have become rich and celebrated, although the action depicted in their crime fiction is (in my opinion) a sort of pornography of violence.

However—ethical or moral considerations aside—I don't perceive that a high degree of sensationalistic, sexually twisted homicidal activity will necessarily sell a novel. Some editors might on occasion buy material of this sort, but the stronger trend is toward seeking to avoid its purchase.

Nearly every mystery will, nonetheless, sooner or later (usually by page 50), feature a killing. How should the writing of that be dealt with?

According to Classification

The violent acts should be handled to subgenre type. Graphic violence—although not of the sadistic kind, such as we discussed above—can be presented when it is appropriate to the overall tone and intention of the novel. If the novel is gritty, even a biker gang rape can be described—again, so long as the presentation is reportorial and not salacious. Stylistically, the gritty mystery is either neutral in feel—like a camera on the seedier side of life—or wryly observing. Adult themes and realistic happenstance do not have to be avoided in mystery fiction, although most mystery fiction, even hardboiled, doesn't present a lot of unadorned street life.

The thing you must do, if this is the type of fiction you choose to write, is to make it good, first of all, and—target your market. Don't send a gritty book to a fiction line that prefers cozy novels. Usually, your agent will make these determinations, but it is possible that you will submit on your own. In such a case, you should spend some time examining recent mystery releases for any that are similar to yours in texture. The publisher(s) issuing these books are the ones to which you should submit.

But most people writing mystery today do not write gritty, so the degree of violence on the page is more likely to be limited. I don't write gritty, myself, but I don't shy away from scenes that contain violence or violent murders. I have a book coming out soon that begins with a violent scene, but the violence doesn't have an especially emotional tone. The killer is a bit repulsed by his own act, in fact, yet he commits the murder with what he considers a "good" motivation. So, although the killing is shown right in front of the reader, unless he/she is especially sensitive, I don't think the scene will cause someone to stop reading. The event presented might be shocking, but it isn't gory. Further, we don't know the murdered character well enough to be distraught.

Most murders in cozy books don't take place on the page at all. The reader may enter the scene and see the body lying askew with a tidily arranged amount of blood on the floor. While the effort, thereafter, is focused completely on tracking the bloke who dun it, the ugliness of the act itself is minimized.

Don't Harm Fido

Just one aside in this discussion of violence, which comes from remarks by a number of readers. People do not like to see pets killed in fiction. That is even more upsetting to them than seeing a person thrown off a cliff. They also do not want to read about any serious harm done to a child. Even gritty crime fiction should be extremely careful in this regard. I myself stopped reading a book I was going to review when a little girl's ear was cut off. The reader was not forced to see it happen, but I gave up when her ear appeared in a box and we next saw the child in bandages. I have yet to understand the point of including this, although I have a scene in one of my books in which the protagonist cuts two people's throats. But they are very, very bad men, and we know it; they are not innocent children who have been tortured and will be miserably maimed for life.

Which brings up the point that if you are going to have your protagonist kill someone, you'd better establish how dreadful that person is. Maybe he/she threatened a child or, worse, a cat.

Torture scenes must be depicted with restraint as well. I don't often see such scenes in mysteries, in fact; nor do I want to. I think they are a mistake, even when used to show how bad the bad guys are. Many, many readers find this type of material unacceptable. Instead of demonstrating torture (which elicits a degree of empathy that changes a fun read to a repellent experience), you might want to show acts from which the victim will obviously recover.

Finally, I recall talking with a number of mystery writers about how people who had been touched by murder in their own families have approached them over the years. The family members cannot comprehend how or why anyone would write a murder mystery; the topic is too raw for them to even contemplate the idea of a murder story as entertainment.

I do believe that most mystery authors understand the seriousness of such crimes and that their intention toward society is to act as a mirror or as shamans—to not simply amuse, but to help, even to heal. I can't, therefore, agree with the overly sensitive point of view, but in writing violence such a consideration should be held in mind. All professionals, even writers, should keep before them the medical model: First Do No Harm.

Aside from a couple of authors I know who use the mystery form to exorcise certain of their own violent tendencies (thus handling their aggression with artistry), most crime fiction writers are entirely horrified by the idea of genuine wrongdoing—although they are really rather interested in crime, too. Murder, after all, isn't only a violent deed; the solving of such a monstrous act is a conundrum to be figured out. Some minds enjoy a puzzle.

Even the gore of the crime—the blood and its components, the substances in it or not in it, the DNA patterns— are a forensic curiosity, too, and not something to be reveled in.

Exercises:

CHOREOGRAPHY NEEDED: Want some punch 'em up? The readers might. Just as love scenes can be tough to create, fight scenes present a challenge as well. In the movies, people choreograph this type of action, which is what you'll have to do to show a fight. Try it—you might enjoy it. If you can't get beyond *Ted punched his attacker,* try to visualize the scene. What part of the bad person's anatomy does Ted strike? What does the attacker do in turn—put his arm up defensively? Think step by step. After this, go back and write in some perceptions of pain. For example, you might first say: *Jerrod blocked the fist aimed at his face and Ted's knuckles struck Jerrod's forearm.* The next time you go through, you can provide the ouch factor: *Ted winced as his knuckles struck the hard bone of Jerrod's forearm.*

DON'T HIDE THE GRIEF: Showing the response to violence or to a murder is not that easy, but nothing is so lame as an emotionless reaction when a body is found or a death reported to a friend. I don't mean for you to be ghoulish, but watch the news—real people react to incidents of horror every night. Show the discovery of the body, the witnessing of the killing, or the reaction to a loved one's demise, recreating the type of real feeling actual people demonstrate.

4

Similar
Offenses

——— MYSTERIES COME IN AN ABBREVIATED FORM ———

For those whose greatest ambition in life is to write mysteries, remember, we can produce other works aside from the crime fiction *novel*.

The first alternative that might come to mind is the short mystery story. Many opinions as to the value of writing the short story exist, but this can be a pathway in your career. I have seen an author sell a short story that won an award (the Short Mystery Fiction Society Derringer) and then go on—at least in part on the basis of that story—to publish a novel that did quite well.

Short stories may be easier to sell than novels, but they aren't a guaranteed sale by any means. Everyone aims for the two top markets—*Ellery Queen Mystery Magazine* and *Alfred Hitchcock Mystery Magazine*—making both these publications more than slightly tough to break into. Moreover, most of the authors in these pages are repeats. By all means submit to these two Dell Magazines' offerings (really owned now by Penny Press) but don't beat yourself up if you fail to receive an acceptance. Be ready with some other markets up your sleeves.

Most of the *AHMM* and *EQMM* stories are rather long, verging on novella length. These are the only periodicals, for the most part, to which you can sell such a long short story. Therefore, if you view the odds with a certain degree of clarity, you might start by writing for some less difficult markets, with several markets in mind at once. The more magazines you send to, the more likely publication is.

Some people don't believe that writing short mystery fiction is profitable. I'm the current president of the Short

Mystery Fiction Society and I think that writing short has definite value. A few writing credentials for stories sold will give you something to put in your cover letter to authors' reps and editors. In fact, when querying in your agent search, short story credentials help prove your worthiness. The competition to get representation is tough and the more edge you have the better! You won't make much money with shorts, but then again, you will gain the pleasant experience of selling, if you persist.

Many authors also say that the forms are so different that those who want to write novels shouldn't bother writing short. I don't believe that, either. A sentence is a sentence and the work of forming and polishing these will hold you in good stead whatever length you later choose.

A few mystery writers actually only write short mysteries—this includes Ed Hoch, the one American who has made a living from writing short mystery stories. He regularly writes for the Dell Magazine Deadly Duo and gains additional revenues from anthologies. Hoch won double acknowledgment in 2001 by being the Bouchercon fan convention's guest of honor and by being named the Mystery Writers of America Grandmaster, the highest status a mystery writer can attain.

Etcetera

Other types of mystery markets exist, from children's mysteries, to young adult mysteries, to screenplays, to plays. Of these, the market I would suggest with the most potential (surprisingly) is the play market. If you have a play that does even moderately well, you can earn royalties from small theater productions across the country. Moreover, there are not many mystery playwrights in action today. You would have a fair shot.

The screenplay, including television plays, on the other hand, is a far more competitive venue. Breaking in is less a matter of just having a good property and more a matter of making the right connections and then having something to offer that stands out. Best of luck.

The children's book arena, including mystery, is nearly as difficult as the market for adult novels. But you can try. If your title finds entrée into the world of the school book fairs, sales can be brisk. Children who have a few dollars in their pocket like to spend them and mystery is a favorite genre with the elementary set. Short mystery stories for youngsters pay well per word, too, if you target the established publications.

You can also aim for the young adult market. Avalon Books, for instance, looks for YA mysteries of about 50,000 words written with adult characters. The books sell well—and just about exclusively—to the school library market. Don't expect much money on the sale though—the imprint pays on the low end.

—— A STRATEGY FOR WRITING THE MYSTERY SHORT ——

A mystery story, or any story, for that matter, begins with a single strong intention: "I will write thus and such." This is the spark behind the act of creation. However, the more vague the sense that one is about to sit down and write a story . . . any day now . . . the less likely that the story will be written.

Oppositely, a specific intention carries with it a great deal of force: "I'm going to write a story for The Bad Versus the Good Mystery Magazine and I'll make it about 3,000 words because that's the length that the editor prefers" is the type of plan that will run its course to completion.

But what is the story going to be about? Not to worry. Stating the intention alone initiates a process that spins the story idea out of thin air. Thinking about The Bad Versus the Good recalls to mind that the editor only accepts hardboiled tales. Now what if the story that you're planning is, sadly, rejected by TBVTG? Will another magazine possibly take a 3,000-word hardboiled story? None you can think of. So, any hardboiled story written with TBVTG in mind would have to be limited to that one market.

Unless . . . Perhaps the editor might take a Mother's Day story because he likes to acknowledge the holidays in the magazine. Further, if he doesn't take the Mother's Day story (which, in honor of the holiday, might squeak by medium-boiled), maybe Mothers in Mystery Magazine would take it . . .

While we don't have the idea for the story yet, exactly, we have a couple of embers.

The Neurons Fire Up

We all have heard the brain likened to a computer and there's a hint of truth to that analogy. In making some choices as to what kind of story we are going to write and by maintaining our aim that we will sit down and write a mystery of 3,000 words for TBVTG magazine, we have launched the neurological "search" function into motion. Our gray matter is looking everywhere for the idea that connects Mother/Mother's Day plus mystery, plus a medium-boiled attitude, and that can have beginning, middle, and end in 3,000 words.

I admit here that I am describing something of my very own process in launching forth to write a short mystery. I have learned over a period of some years that you shouldn't just settle at the keyboard and write, willy-nilly. That's how you wind up with stories you might like, but that don't actually sell. Writing with at least more than one market in mind gives the story some better potential of ending up in print.

On the other hand, I know that there are writers who have only one style or even subject. That's the mood they evoke every time they settle in to form a story, novel, or whatever. The decision of how boiled the story should be, or any such consideration, never comes to mind. And that's fine. If you're one of those people, that part of the process is already eliminated. Go on from there.

The tip here is to narrow the definition of the story little by little, then mull over what the story is going to be. This mulling is a very important step in the writing of the mystery story; the author has to undergo some process of thought.

In drafting a novel, you can continue to think about the plot over time, as you work. A short story has to be a bit more concrete in the writer's mind before the writing commences. You might not need to know every twist and turn of the story, but having the basics in place can be very helpful. And there's no other way to arrive at the main story points—start, development with a couple of mini-climaxes (perhaps a surprise reversal), and conclusion—but by thinking directly on the question.

Gee, but why make such a big deal about this thinking

business? Isn't that a given, something that goes along automatically with every activity in life? Yes, but not entirely. Automatic thinking is like shedding skin cells—it happens every second we're alive, even during the night when we're asleep. But automatic thinking usually isn't creative thinking, the type of thought required to craft a plot.

An initial idea will come from the programmed subconscious, but beyond that, the writer needs to mold the storyline while concentrating directly on the inquiries arising from plot construction. Concentration, in this phase, is the key. Automatic thinking is stream of consciousness. The stream is there and it flows on. No effort is required to move along. Creative work, on the other hand, is just that—work. The attention must be held in place, plot possibilities thought out with some dedication, and so forth.

To put the above in other terms—even though one part of the brain is in computer mode, scratching through the subconscious for bits of ideas that fit the circumstance, another part of the brain has to be consciously employed to set the material into a form that resembles a short mystery tale.

Finally, the plot is shaped—not filled in, necessarily, but outlined mentally. Now, the work operation shifts to sitting at the keyboard and giving form to all of these ideas and the movement of the skeletal story. Words have to be hung from the conception.

Story Inhabitants

While plot gives you the structure, the characters give you the point of interest for your readers. People, after all, are interested in others of their ilk. So, in order to arouse real reader enthusiasm, the characters have to be given a vivid, lifelike existence. Although often in short mystery, the writer chooses the perpetrator as the protagonist, I'd suggest that a sympathetic figure is more likely to keep an audience reading. Have you ever heard a reviewer or critic say, "There was no one to identify with?" We want our empathy to be held— not just our minds. *How I Killed Aunt May* is never a story that I have found gripping. More intriguing (to me) is the tale of a protagonist's struggles to expose Aunt May's killers. Give me someone I can root for and I'm all yours.

How then, do you sketch a person in words? Physical description? That's a start, but do it from the inside. *Her arthritic bones protested as she climbed the stairs* can be more effective than showing an older character's crow's feet or facial lines. However, sags and bags, too, can be approached with greater impact than the usual. *The stranger studied Nelly's face, while she watched him in turn. Did he think he could read her thoughts in the crosshatches that ran from the corners of her eyes? She smiled, creasing her face further still.* Here, in addition to the exterior image, you also get a picture of the character's internal existence, which is where the real protagonist creation comes from. We know something about this older woman already: She is observant and intelligent, but additionally has a pleasant aspect and a certain self-objectivity.

The bringing to life of secondary characters is a little bit different. These characters are mostly observed from outside their heads. Although you can enter into the secondary character's viewpoint, I'd advise that you do not attempt any point of view switches in a very short story. POV shifts are tricky and best left alone until you clearly understand and have a good purpose for them.

In writing the secondary character, again, active description is better than passive. We could say, *The stranger was large,* but let's try something else: *He loomed over her so that his bulk cast a shadow, depriving her of the warming sun.* The emotional context in this particular quote implies that the man is sinister. If we have already established the protagonist's arthritis, the sentence details the effect of this man on her well being.

Should you then calculate every little piece of description, "deciding" that the protagonist has arthritis and that the secondary character will somehow bother her because of her ailment? No! That's what the computer brain, or intuitive reflex, of the author, is for. Once you have established for yourself who the character is and how she feels, you will automatically find ways to use that information. That's what writing the story is about.

Development

A short story, very much like a novel, has an "arc" that consists of an ascent, a peak at a little past the halfway point, and a descent. The exact delineation of the arc can vary, but we must have this sequence of ascent, culmination/climax, and resolution. The manner in which this is performed is called "pacing" and the storywriter's pacing is either ept or inept. Pacing is dictated by the nature of the story itself.

To go back, we've set a 3,000-word parameter. This isn't going to be a long, long story, so we won't plan to send the hero on a trip from New Jersey to Africa. We simply don't have enough time. In fact, the story will probably take place all in one locale, or, at least, a limited number. Setting the story in the chosen background will take a few words itself.

Maybe not that many. *Another boringly beautiful day in Paradise—Paradise, Florida, in fact—and Jeb, obeying the summons of the sun, was on his way to play his usual round of golf.* Twenty-nine words. Let's cut to the chase. *Was on his way, that is, until he saw the dead man lying in the road.* Perhaps more setting. *Paradise was a town of minuscule proportions, so Jeb figured he must know the corpse.*

Everything that happens next can flow out of what has been said in that first paragraph, along with our pre-writing, plotting work. Events progress from the logic of the facts we've set down, once we begin to paint-in the situation. We "discover" the nitty-gritty story development.

In fact, my concluding that Jeb must have been acquainted with the murdered man in life springs from the knowledge that Paradise is not the name of a familiar Florida city. The town is obviously a very small one; therefore, the protagonist must have, at some time, met the corpse. Here's a crossroads. Did he know the dead man or not? If so, one set of proceedings will occur, based on what people will naturally do and think. Or, if he doesn't know the man, then another set of circumstances will arise. Writing the events of the story are as simple as that—simpler, since you know the outcome and where you want to arrive, a mere 2,915 words or so later.

Voila, THE END

The ending to the short mystery should be in tune with the type of story you have written and the characters you have created. Again, think about the pacing. The story arc demands that the ending not be too abrupt. Just as there was a build to the highpoint, there is a build to the conclusion—

although this "build" is on the down slope of the arc. We not only need to find out what happens in the end—we need to understand the ramifications. How have people's lives been changed by what occurred here, and especially by the solution of the mystery? That's a lot to pack into 3,000 words, but for a story to work better than a mere rattletrap for plot, the impact phase is necessary.

Can you write a short mystery from reading the above meditation? Only if you make the ingredients your own, adapting my advice to your own artistic approach. Will you do it? Do you have the talent? Yes, if you've maintained the interest to read this far, I guarantee you will and do. I wish you the best of outrageous fortune—and lots of fun.

Exercises:

ANOTHER OPENING: You can build an entire plot on logic alone. Write a few opening paragraphs and then write the stories. Oh, too much work? I was only kidding. Pick one and outline the story, trying to feel your way along, using everyday common sense. Each detail in the opening will lead to some conclusions for a story. A story set in winter, for example, will give both the bank robbers and the cops a different set of problems. Use the specifics in the paragraph to develop the plot. Feel like writing the whole piece now?

IT'S A BUSINESS: Writing mystery isn't only fun—you can publish and make money. Go to a newsstand or the magazine section at your local bookstore and see what magazines contain mystery. This might easily include a literary publication or two. Stand there and examine the writing until the management kicks you out. Now look for *Novel and Short Story Writer's Market* from Writer's Digest Books. Best bet, break down and buy the book. Otherwise, at least check on the guidelines for the magazine that interests you most. Oh, I forgot; this isn't an exercise. This is what we do in real life. Now write the story.

———— FIVE SPECIFIC CLUES TO THE CRIME BRIEF ————

One of the failings of most short mysteries published today is the sameness of style—as if these stories were all formed by the identical, generic story cutter. Don't strive to write based on the model that these authors are using, please! Follow a few clues, listed here, and do it your way—differently.

1. LOCATION, LOCATION, LOCATION: Or, I could say, setting, setting, setting. Whether you select a physical locale that is exotic and compelling, a little-known historical period, or an unusual background industry, making a unique and intriguing choice will automatically transform your story. While it is said that there is nothing new under the sun, placing your characters in India during a cataclysmic earthquake can give you a very different scrim against which to sculpt a riveting story. The reader is automatically interested in a topic that represents such an overwhelming life drama.

Or don't use India, if you feel it's too late to research the event. Pick up today's newspaper and see what catches your attention. Enough is going on across the globe that will provide a mesmerizing accompaniment to your basic plot and characters. The research has already been done for you in that tabloid's articles. Add a few details by searching online and you will have a piece that no one else can possibly offer.

2. PEOPLE ARE COMPLEX: Rather than inserting the generic

burglar or standard elderly female character, try to remember that there is no excuse to be predictable when it comes to human personality traits. How about mixing and matching characteristics for some surprises? For instance, why not give us a little old lady burglar? But, for goodness sake, don't make her cute. Think Lauren Hutton as the grandmotherly burglar, or Elizabeth Dole. Maybe your Dole figure is breaking into the Watergate Apartments for information that will help a charitable organization like the Red Cross?

3. PEOPLE AREN'T CARDBOARD: Character is too important a story ingredient to let it go simply by combining disparate elements. Even if you use non-stereotypical outer aspects of those who populate your tales, please also remember to give these beings some actual depth. Assuming that you, as a real human soul, have certain musings and motivations beyond the superficial, so should your short story's cast. While in life, people might kill, in most cases they cite reasons beyond the "she insulted my hybrid roses" theme. Make us believe that there is a strong enough rationale here. Give us a mindset that will chill us, if you like, but don't allow the readers' eyes to roll upward in skepticism or disgust. People are interesting. Characters who aren't true to life are boring.

4. PLOT ELEMENTS SHOULD BE OF THIS WORLD: A person with an everyday education should be able to reasonably assume that a character such as you describe, of this social class and gender and in this setting, will take the action that you, the author, have ordained. While a complex character doesn't have to act exactly to type (see above) a complete absurdity will be taken as such.

Sure, you might want to manipulate the plot to give a twist that will come out of left field, but if you do so, be certain that the reaction is not, "Huh? No way." Too often a plot wrinkle rests on the author's desire to wrinkle the plot and nothing more. Plot has to move from the foundation of what has been set in motion at the start. A twist intended to elicit an "Oh! Wow!" (not that "Huh?") must be an unthought-of surprise, not a dumb ploy.

5. ADD YOURSELF TO THE STORY: In other words, personalize the story to the greatest extent possible. That's what authorship, in the end, is all about. Add your own humor, your own sense of word usage, your own means of emotional expression. A story is not simply backdrop, characters, and plot, it is a work of artistic creation. Words constitute the hues of the writer's pallet, and the magic to be drawn across the canvas is something individual and, heretofore, unknown. Spread those colors as only *you* are able. That is the most essential ingredient in the mix.

Exercises:

GO FOR THE FLASH: One popular short story form is the flash mystery—often under 1,000 words, but certainly under 1,500. You will find many publication venues for these short shorts and many even pay. Moreover, the quality doesn't have to be literary since the emphasis is on the plot. Sit down and structure one or two with a twist at the end. Then write and polish, polish, polish. Now submit. The submission is part of the "exercise."

EVERY WORD COUNTS: One factor in writing the short story is the word count for your target publication. Practice cutting word by word, which is a great skill to own for all occasions. Write a story, save that version, now cut for another market you have in mind. Submit both pieces.

5

Getting the Story Straight

Now, Maximize Your Writing Sizzle

The markets for selling our fiction are tough ones. The majority of spots within mainstream publishing go to name writers. The few opportunities that remain at the large mystery publishers—and the single-digit chances at each of the small presses—will be won by writers who can maximize their work. Even the much-talked-about e-markets are extremely selective and difficult to crack. Weak writing will not make the cut, despite the hype by vested interests that these e-publishers are so indiscriminate.

The best way to establish a career in crime fiction—or other genre fiction for that matter—is to improve your writing skills so that your stories clearly stand out from the pack.

I am going to try to help you do that in this section of the book. Don't be discouraged if you begin to see a few of your faults. We all have areas in which our limitations appear to rule. The only way to overcome these flaws and to become the writers we dream of being is to look at our current inabilities and correct them. Knowing where our deficiencies lie can sometimes be painful, but if we are serious about our craft, what a blessing!

No stylistic defects exist that cannot be changed into writing strengths. A tendency to throw in excess verbiage is not like a genetic prescription for stubby little toes. We can learn to slenderize our writing, even if, despite all the pulling we do, we still have feet that don't measure up.

I can't guarantee that by the end of these pages, you will write like Dostoevsky (why, you probably don't even know the Russian language), but you will have seen a few things in your word use that you can improve.

A wise woman who lived in India (the Mother) once wrote that there are two quite opposite illusions we simultaneously hold about ourselves and our ambitions. First of all, we believe that our urge to step in a direction is identical with our completion of the aim. We don't see that years of effort are required to develop the necessary underpinnings. Secondly, and at the same time, we don't really believe that we have the ability to fulfill our longed-for goals.

We are wrong on both counts, the Mother says. We consider our achievements with too great a complacency, but we really lack confidence. We think we'll never make the grade. The desire itself, however—while it isn't the accomplishment—is a strong indicator that the capacity for eventual success lies within. Let's take our inborn ability as a given, and unwaveringly move toward the hoped-for end destination—becoming the writer we know is inside of us.

Exercises:

Want to maximize your prose and make it sing? Try these exercises:

To Be or Not To Be—That Is the Question: The answer is "No!" Try avoiding the "was," "am," and "is" forms of "to be" and, instead, use a verb that adds some zest. You might need to compound your sentences to do this. For instance:

Laura was a lovely girl, as beautiful inside as out. She was also intelligent and had been well-educated by her parents.

That's not so bad, but, how about:

A lovely and educated young woman, Laura radiated a deep inner beauty out of dark, intelligent, shining eyes.

I like the second way of describing Laura better, although

the sentence might not be perfect yet. Why should it be? I haven't reworked it more than a few times. Word choice for impact requires repeated effort.

I'm not saying to never use the verb "to be" or its various forms. However, try ways of expressing your meaning other than merely letting a passive (to be) verb lie on the page without punch.

WE HEARD YOU THE FIRST TIME: Do not repeat words, even for emphasis. What you view currently as placing a pleasing focus on a word sound may later strike you as an unnecessary repetition. Not only do you have a thesaurus on your word processor, you can rephrase an expression or word entirely to avoid duplication.

Naked he came into the world and naked he left might turn into:

Naked he came into the world and, by the time of his exit, he had been stripped bare of every stitch of comprehension, affection, and possession he had, in his 30-some years of life, acquired.

I like the second form better because this phrasing adds concepts and information. You might prefer the first for the simplicity it conveys, but try the exercise anyway. Here's another example:

He loved her passionately. He loved her to the depths of life itself might become: *His worship of her knew no limits. His love sprang from the core of all that lived within his depths.*

Practice each one of these exercises a couple of times, at least. When you next sit down to work on a project, remember what you did and see if you can use the exercises, to some degree, in your writing.

──────── Sweating on a Chain Gang ────────

You guys do the work in this chapter. Me, I'm heading for a snooze.

Exercises:

Pump Up the Volume: Exaggerate your words to the extreme. While this definitely should be employed as an exercise only, practice of this type might help those who have trouble with vivid communication. Often, we think a word is too bold when the choice might convey exactly the force needed at that spot.

He hit her on the head and escaped into the wood might become *He smashed at her with the bit of ancient granite clutched within his tightly bound fist. Recoiling in terror of the consequences, Mark snarled out a few savage syllables, then fled to the sheltering security of the nearby forest.*

While I don't truly like overdone wording, more vivid writing grabs editors who are on the lookout for books with popular appeal.

Or, in other words, "While I despise sentences that mercilessly howl for the readers' attention, these grating shrieks often elicit an editor's fervent commercial grasping."

Yikes. Maybe, in the end, we can find a compromise form of communication.

The exercise succeeds though because you will soon see that many times the words you use are simply too bland.

Now Emote: Write some paragraphs with the prime emphasis on the characters' feelings. Readers watch to see how the people in a story feel. Even though that might not be the only element of the narrative you want to emphasize, this exercise will help you be alert to the emotional aspect of your words. Without some focus on feeling, a novel can't be brought to life.

Here's the example—taking a paragraph from my own work that never got any further than this start:

Chicken stewing in coconut milk wafted a delicious odor throughout the house. Lucy stirred and added a cup of chopped mango, a cup of chopped coconut, and a table-spoon of chili peppers when, suddenly, the doorbell rang. She swore mildly under her breath, rowed the wooden spoon quickly through the ingredients, and grabbed a paper towel to wipe her hands.

Doing the exercise, I change the above to this:

Lucy was absolutely starving, which fueled an irritability that mounted as she cooked. The chicken stewing in coconut milk smelled delicious, but how furious she was that the ingredients had cost so much. Lucy fretted, an anxiety gnawing at her already clenched-tight belly. Tears sprang to her eyes at the thought of her terrifying financial situation. She felt that she would certainly go mad.

The doorbell rang sending a chill of apprehension up her spine. She cursed whomever had come hounding her. The threatened tears spilled over at last and she broke into sobs. How she hated them all, the lucky ones.

Gee, I guess this won't be a romance novel, after all. But maybe I ought to cheer Lucy up. Today could be the best day of her life.

Lucy couldn't resist breaking into a favorite salsa lyric as she peppered her chicken stew with a tablespoon of hot green chilies. How utterly and unreasonably joyous she was. She had breathlessly anticipated this very day for months. Tears sprang to her eyes and she grinned at her own absurdity. Would she ever feel this marvelously alive again?

The doorbell rang and a flush rose to her cheeks. At the same time, she shivered in anticipation. Had there ever been a happier woman than she?

True that neither of these was the story I had started to write. But perhaps one of these openings would make a more exciting project.

'IT'-LESS IN WORD LAND: Don't begin your sentences with the word 'it.' I have been working on this exercise quite a bit recently and I have become very conscious of the 'it' problem. Although sometimes 'it' may be the subject of a sentence, not only is the word badly overused, sentences avoiding 'it' often have much more power. Try working this way; you'll like living 'it'-free.

Here's an example:

It was the best of times; it was the worst of times. Oh, hell, not that one—let's leave Charles Dickens alone.

Here's the actual example for you:

Nancy should have known that her Tuesday would turn sour when it took her 20 minutes to leave the bank parking lot that morning. It was not the idyllic day off she had hoped for and she was irked—especially since it was her one free day this season.

Her near collision with another car served as a strong reminder of why she had to quit her job. It was no accident that she never had an opportunity for relaxation. It was much easier for the bosses to insist on the necessity of overtime than for them to hire an extra worker.

Too many 'it's! Try rewriting these paragraphs, varying the words and sentence forms to create a more vivid and engaging effect. Bring the more important portion of the sentence forward—where the forceful element actually belongs.

Again, just indulge me and give these a try.

———— EIGHT COMMON WRITER MISDEMEANORS ————

Although writers—even famous ones—commit an endless range of verbal atrocities on a daily basis, the following are a few that you can seek and destroy in your own work.

1. INEXPRESSIVE PHRASING: Expression in fiction must be *articulated* expression. Produce a vivid picture for the reader through economical but lively wording:

The woman stepped forward into the big room. Her dress was long and white. The sleeves hung down with ruffles at each end.

I would call this writing inexpressive and flat, despite the effort to describe the dress. In fact, that's part of the problem here. The dress doesn't have to be described to such extent and with so little result. *A young, oval-faced woman in a long, white dress stepped into the ballroom* would just about say it all. Later, when she dances with a stranger, the ruffles on her sleeves can brush his cheek.

The best approach to description is to condense the image and integrate the details with the action.

Sometimes writing seems empty because the writer has nothing to say. This happens when there is a lack of focus within the scene, or novel overall. Drama can only be heightened when the stage is set for conflict. The characters must have motivation in every scene. Their passionate drive toward an eagerly sought goal ought to help invigorate the writing.

2. INDEFINITE WORDS AND PHRASING: *In the park, families, children, and couples in love were walking, playing or just enjoying the sun on this Sunday afternoon. The worst heat of the day was already over.*

This isn't so bad, but I'd like to see more specific detail instead of walking, playing, or just enjoying. Further, what kind of families? How do we know the couples are in love? We want to SEE the scene.

In the park, two tow-headed toddlers in blue bathing trunks dipped in the lake by the skimpy, six-foot-long sand beach. A mother, pulling strands of blonde hair away from her sweating face, watched indulgently and called out cautions and encouragement. A short, stocky Hispanic male passed, tugging at a stubborn white pit bulldog that strained to be off after its own pursuits . . .

We don't actually know where the author is going with the scene, so we don't know how broad or how limited the description should be. Nonetheless, the scene should be set with a couple of definite, albeit unobtrusive, images.

3. USE OF INDEFINITE PRONOUNS: The writer should make the narrative perfectly and explicitly clear in all respects. Yes, readers will probably understand what you are trying to say, anyway, with your pronouns. But why force them to labor so hard at what should be easy? Make them work at understanding a characterization that is subtly drawn, not at comprehending the meaning of the words. Here are a couple of examples:

The owl winged noiselessly across the moon's path and settled on an oak bough above his head. He didn't look up.

Yes, we know that the second creature in the description is a man, but the reference is still indefinite and not sufficient. Why not go ahead and say: *above the man's head*? Or, if possible, name the man. More experienced, polished writers write as precisely as they can.

No woman had ever dared set foot inside. A giant Nubian doorman made certain of that. Here, he and his friends could cast off society's cloying inhibitions. Here, they were free.

Yes, we are aware that the "he" is not the doorman, and the goof isn't grievous, but the author should have used the character's name instead of the "he," after the intervening discussion of a different character.

Black smoke hung thick in the air. Near the ground, visibility was less than one half mile. Most of the oil wells had been torched by Saddam Hussein's retreating army. It was the closest resemblance to Hell that the men could imagine.

"It" is always a dangerous word to use, as we've discussed; yet "it" is used more than any other subject word in the English language. Sometimes the meaning is entirely obvious. In this example, the "it" is not linked to a specific preceding reference at all. The author truly ought to have said, *The resulting scene more closely resembled Hell than any earthly setting that the men could imagine*, or some such. Yes, the rest of the paragraph would probably change. But that's all right. That is part of the process of self-editing and comes from an appreciation for the texture of the language.

4. IMPRECISE OR INEPT PHRASING: This flaw is similar to the above. Here, again, readers are left to make their own deduction about meaning. Some examples:

A golden moonlight washed over an olive Range Rover racing with pegged speedometer across a lifeless stretch

of tarred two-lane highway. Carved out of a barren land-
scape, the trunk provided the only overland connection
between Kaduna in central Nigeria and Kano in the north-
ern territory.

I don't know what a pegged speedometer is, but I'm willing to acknowledge that might be my own fault. What I do
object to here is the use of the word trunk, when "trunk
road" should be fully stated. If the entire phrase is not
employed, the reader's mind might wander to the trunk of
the car in which we are racing.

Robbery and murder prevailed here like the giant ter-
mite mounds standing sentry along the way.

This is an example of inept phrasing. Even if much of the
imagery created by the author is admirable, I don't understand why robbery and murder are "like" giant termite
mounds, although both "prevail." The two ends of the analogy do not match up, despite the author's effort to force
them together. I like the image of the giant termite mounds,
which is very graphic and startling, but the author might
simply have said: *Giant termite mounds stood sentry along*
the way in describing the road and then, later, he could have
announced, *Robbery and murder prevailed here.* That
would have foreshadowed nicely what I assume will come
next in the story.

The following sentence qualifies as inept: *As he automat-*
ically operated the controls, the pilot was caught up in the
very same thoughts that have occupied warriors for gener-
ations—coup.

I honestly have no comprehension of what the pilot had
on his mind. I know what a coup is, but the preceding sentences do not tell me either why he was thinking of a coup

or why warriors always think in those terms. I have written about soldiers and sailors myself—even pilots—and I'm at a loss.

Two last examples of inept, imprecise turns of phrase:

It had been more than six months since my last ciga-rette, so my wife, Felicity, was none too excited when I decided to revive my old habit of cigar smoking.

I'd guess that Felicity was probably very much excited—she simply wasn't overly happy.

The young man gave a perceptible nod.

If the nod was perceptible, then the author should say, *The young man nodded*. Otherwise, the nod was *just barely perceptible* or *almost imperceptible*.

5. EXCESS AND OVERLY DETAILED VERBIAGE: Here's an example: *At the heart of the County, bounded to the west by a frozen Hackensack Reservoir, to the east by a well-sanded Fells Point Road, and to the north and south by lines born of the surveyor's pencil, was the Borough of Lyme. Near the cen-ter of town, halfway up steep and slippery Watkins Hill, just opposite the upper exit of the Lyme Elementary School, lived Henrietta Masty.*

Why is this excess verbiage? Really, simply because we cannot connect to it. To be honest, reading the above makes me dizzy. The author wrote from the head and not from the heart. He or she knows this area extremely well, but the rest of us don't. The details pile up fast and furious. There are too many place names. Give us a break.

Now contrast this with the elegant (though flawed) writ-ing of Sarah Orne Jewett (1849-1909) in The Country of the Pointed Firs.

There was something about the coast town of Dunnet

which made it seem more attractive than other maritime vil-
lages of eastern Maine. Perhaps it was the simple fact of
acquaintance with that neighborhood which made it so
attaching, and gave such interest to the rocky shore and
dark woods and the few houses which seemed to be
securely wedged and tree-nailed in among the ledges by
the Landing.

We might also not know this geographic region, but the detailing is anchored to emotion and is not just a stream of place names.

Make an effort to avoid overloading the reader and giving too much, too soon. Although providing some narrative facts at the start of your story is a good idea—like an establishing shot in film or television—try to be sparing. We want to know what you have to say, but we are not mere brains at the other side of the writing process waiting to be fed a bunch of data.

6. OVERLY FLORID WRITING: While writing that's too plain or flat doesn't fly, neither will description that is too flowery. Poetic phrasing is nice for emphasis, but don't try to make every stitch of your writing stand out. That type of overblown narrative is silly, at best.

Turning, he struck the end of a wooden fireplace match,
bringing it to life, and as the flame settled to evenness,
merged it with the wick of a yellow votive candle resting in
a homemade stand . . .

Okay, there's something nice about the effort, but the action itself isn't worth the focus. How about: *He lit the yellow votive candle with a fireplace match.* That's our contemporary style—straightforward and factual, easy to read. If we want to add more lyrical writing, we can do that at a moment in the story that warrants special attention.

By the way, those wanting to read a powerful story written in entirely simple language should try to find Elia Kazan's *America, America*. Kazan, the idolized as well as reviled Hollywood director, has written in other styles, but chose plain wording to tell the story of his family's immigration to the United States. He made a wonderful film from the novel as well. If you want to see how economy of language can work in writing, this is the book to read.

7. PASSIVE WRITING: Don't yield to the temptation to use the passive forms of verbs or any type of equivocation. To the extent possible, state what you have to express in an active and direct form.

It was that fact that had led to Rumlar being chosen as the counsel who would guide Mosdark in his attempts to regain his power.

Lose the passive voice: *Based on these qualifications, Rumlar now guided Mosdark. With Rumlar's help, the Lord of the Invisible World would regain his power.*

"No one would have thought they could betray you and survive."

"None of the citizens [be specific] *could have betrayed you and survived."*

8. UNGRAMMATICAL WRITING: Oh no. We must not fracture the English language—most of the time. Sometimes we do break the rules to make the language less stiff. But the following examples are simply mistakes.

The crew of the AH-64 Apache attack helicopter were on their second sortie for the day—if it could be called day."

The crew *was* on *its* second sortie of the day.

Less than a mile from her destination, the Honda suddenly sputtered and slowed. Alice slammed the heel of her hand on the steering wheel. The needle of the gas gauge was past E. "Dammit!" she shouted as the car coasted to a stop.

Do we know for sure the Honda is a she? The entire first phrase modifies the Honda. Therefore, the author ought to have used Alice's name, or said: *Less than a mile from her destination, Alice felt the Honda suddenly sputter and slow.* I like that better, anyway, as the subject of the paragraph is Alice and her reactions, not the car itself.

It was Annie that felt out of place.

Nope, Annie is a *who* not a *that.*

The moon was full shedding light on the ring of stones.

This is a fine example of why we use commas. *The moon was full, shedding light on the ring of stones.*

Her family had not known what to do with her, had finally admitted that nothing could be done, and at the age of ten, had left her to be forgotten within its cold walls.

If her family was only ten, no wonder they couldn't take care of her. (That could be changed to *when she was ten.*) Moreover, this seems to say that the family has cold walls. I don't think so.

The round room started to feel as if it was closing in.

We can never even begin to guess how the room felt as it rarely speaks. *The walls seemed to close in on her.*

Exercises:

KEEP YOUR EYES OPEN: Keep the above list of writing weaknesses beside you when you read. Spot any goofs? Good. You'll be able to pick them out in your own writing.

RUTHLESS SELF-CRITICISM: Now take an objective peek

at your own recent work. Can you be convicted of any of these unprintable offenses?

—————————— LOGICAL CONSISTENCY COUNTS ——————————

Writing comprises many layers of expression, from plot to character, to sequence of sentences. Although solid logic of thought is not the sole ingredient in writing success, an ability to see the story and action in a step-by-step and rational manner can help create a competent—or better—work of fiction. Wild imagination and high-concept plotlines may also assist, but the communication of this extravagance ought to occur in a disciplined fashion.

Those who aren't naturally linear thinkers can learn to concentrate on detail to the extent of being able to write somewhat analytically. In fact, the practice is a good one for developing a faculty of mind that enhances ordinary, everyday life. Learning to be more consistent and less impulsive in one's actions is a positive part of personal development.

When we write, logic is a constant requirement. In fact, reasoning alone can mold a storyline. Employing a systematic method of deduction, an author can take a scrap of character description or an opening image and spin out a reasonable conjecture as to what might occur next. This brainstorming is of the "what if" type, which truly epitomizes creative thought in fiction. "What if," in some sense, is the basis for every fiction narrative ever written.

But the requirement for logical consistency in writing a short story or novel goes beyond plotting and runs well across the board. Here are some applications that you may consider as basic rules to which you must adhere. Simply by paying attention to each as you write, you will increase that proficiency of mind mentioned before: the skill of the person performing a craft; the talent for genuine mindfulness about what you are doing; and the ability to write consciously, and more exactly.

1. LOGICAL CONSISTENCY IN PLOT: One of the annoyances to readers that will make them drop your book like a hot potato is inconsistency within the plot. The plot has to make sense every step of the way and come together at the end without requiring vast mental leaps. The kind of question readers ask is, "Well, why didn't she just leave him when he told her xyz?" The author has to anticipate this very objection and build a rationale into the story. *Katherine was not only a dependent person, but she relied on James exclusively. Moreover, James had control of all the family money.* That's the logic of why Katherine had to protect James by killing Arthur.

Being consistent in plotting doesn't mean you have to pre-plot every little detail. You simply have to remember what you said and then not run counter to your own statements. How do you do that? By keeping in mind that this tracking of plot detail is one of your jobs.

If you later find you've goofed and have to change a situation in the plot, go back and rearrange to straighten out the error. Don't leave inconsistencies. Their existence points to the fact that we're reading fiction and that the plot is a contrivance. Deep down, of course, we know all that—but don't remind us. You'll spoil the illusion.

2. LOGICAL CONSISTENCY IN OVERALL STORY DETAILS: In movie making, the production company employs a "script girl" to watch for logical consistency throughout each scene filmed.

If the star wears a red dress in the first shots of the scene, the script girl must make a notation so that the same dress is worn in every subsequent take. All details must be compatible.

Writing a novel can take even longer than making a film (although not necessarily) and along the way we easily forget the names of the characters and some of their attributes—not to mention location of the action, or what type of beverage is to be found in the refrigerator.

As with all other aspects of logical flow and consistency, don't expect the editor to be your script girl. The editor no longer plays that particular role. Although a line editor who goes over the manuscript will often find these flaws, your work is supposed to be nearly perfect by the time of your submission.

As you read through your novel for a second and third time, even a fourth, you should be alert to the possibility of error and find these bugaboos. Now is the time to catch all blunders—before the novel reaches the galley stage.

3. LOGICAL CONSISTENCY IN CHARACTER: As I re-drafted an old manuscript of mine recently, I came across a gaffe in describing my character. Uh-oh. One minute she was overly tenderhearted and the next she declared that empathy wasn't her strong suit. If I want to send the work out again (and I do), I have to repair Helen's motivation for taking time with an old man in the first instance—so that we understand she wants information, she isn't just being soft. If I don't alter the narrative, the reader will ultimately be confused. Is Helen compassionate and concerned for others' feelings or not? (She's a little self-involved.)

The reader has to be able to trust the author's authority in order to become immersed in the story. To create that trust, you must write real and believable characters, which starts with descriptions that don't contradict one another. Not only does Jane have to be a redhead in *all* her appearances, her behavior has to conform to that of the type of person you declare her to be. If she's a conservative dresser, she only wears a bikini under duress (which could create a very cute scene for some romance).

The important thing though is not just to recall the particulars about your people, but to really know your characters. Who they are isn't always evident to the author early in the story, however. This can take a couple of chapters at least. Often, when you go back through for another draft, you will have to fix a good many comments to comply with the way your characters have developed later on. This minor snafu is natural and not something over which to fret. You might have to write the biography of every character before you begin the novel—many authors do just that. Not every writer wants to or needs to, however, as it isn't much fun. The fun comes in discovery. Just be sure you backtrack eventually and amend the inconsistencies.

4. LOGICAL CONSISTENCY IN SEQUENCE OF ACTION: Most of us who view the story in our mind's eye will see the moment-to-moment flow of activity. The little girl hugs the dog goodbye, then her mother takes the child's hand and they walk off. That's the progression of events and we place them in that order. But some writers might not see what happens in a visual display or, if they do, they see static images. Thus the step-by-step proceeding gets out of synchronization on the page.

This gap of logic in writing action usually occurs at the sentence level. I don't mean that a character shoots, then picks up the gun, exactly, because that's rather obvious. But,

I do see text that reads something like: *The maid left the room. Her attention was on the furniture she dusted, not the woman who sat there in thought.*

We know that the maid didn't come back into the room, but that the writer mistakenly inverted the action because the tableaux was not envisioned clearly. That's okay. But if you know this to be your problem, you must look at all your moment-to-moment sequences and check to be sure they are logical simply on a mental level.

Writers also err in the logic of action on a larger level. I certainly have read manuscripts in which, for instance, a woman calls to rent a car, does a few things, then calls to rent a car. I know of one book in print in which a character also commits the same action twice! Obviously these errors should have been picked up during copyediting. Try to follow the *action* of your story or novel, not just the words, when you undertake your second, then third, draft.

5. LOGICAL CONSISTENCY IN WORDS: Logical consistency in words means that you know what you are saying, which isn't always the case. Here are some examples of this type of verbal mistake:

The woman's head jerked the slightest bit up as she opened her eyes and looked to her left where the voice had come from.

Try to keep verb parts together—as in j*erked up the slightest bit*. Except that this, actually, doesn't need the *up* at all. *Jerked the slightest bit* is sufficient.

Some were less dancing and more watching her, anyway.

Oops. This could be a called a grammatical mistake. *Some of those on the floor watched her more than they actually danced* might work.

She moved over to the strewn body of the Commander.
Strewn can't be employed as an adjective. *Bodies were strewn all over the area* is fine, because strewn is a verb, but you can't say *the strewn bodies were collected by the forensics technicians.*

Be sure of your word use. You can't win, however. A reviewer once incorrectly accused me of a typo or a word misuse. I had written, *He dandled the baby.* She thought I meant that the character *dangled* the baby. Not my character. He truly dandled the little thing. (Never correct a reviewer, by the way.)

No particular exercise will aid you in developing logical consistency in any of these areas. You have to first find out that you have a problem. Then and only then, you can compensate for that mental gap. If you are aware of what your problems are, you can look for and correct the errors in your writing. We all have at least a few failings as writers; mindful effort is what helps us overcome them.

To Vary Forms Is Very Important

What could be more boring than a lack of variation? Nothing. For those of you trying to add excitement to your narrative at the level of the words, remember always to avoid repetition of your sentence formulations. Be conscious of how you set up your sentences and try to break any patterns you overuse or patterns that emerge within paragraphs or approximate vicinity.

Here are a few typical overly repeated structures you can watch for in your writing.

1. THE OVERUSE OF GERUNDS: The gerund is a very popular construction comprising a verb with an 'ing' added so that the word can be used in a dependent clause. For example:

Swimming toward shore, Denise thought with grief about those who hadn't survived the wreck. At last, arriving on dry land, she staggered to her feet. Coming toward her was a burly, half-dressed man.

Those "ing" words are all gerund forms. The form itself can be a nice means of combining thoughts and making sentences more economical, but some who use the verb-as-modifier tend to overuse the construction. Simply be aware when you employ this type of phrase and try to use it well and sparingly. Do not bore the reader's mental ear.

2. THE REPEATED USE OF OTHER SAME-TYPE SENTENCE CONSTRUCTIONS: Using the same construction for many sentences close together produces a droning effect, whether the construction is simple or complex.

He sat next to her and gave her the ring. She blushed and slipped the diamond on her finger. He smiled and leaned over to kiss her.

Nothing is ungrammatical in this paragraph, but after one or two sentences similarly formed, the pattern becomes more noticeable than the meaning of the words.

One step you can take is to vary the length of your sentences. If you have two long sentences, throw in a short one. And so on.

Also keep in mind that a more intricate configuration does not exempt the sentences from producing a "noise" created by the patterning.

Supposedly, he would have gone, but his mother had kept him at home. Luckily, Sally didn't count on him, but had asked Henry at the very last minute.

These are exaggerations, of course, and we may be too experienced to write exactly that way. From time to time, however, we will fall into repeated sentence construction. Let's be on the lookout for any such glitch.

3. THE USE OF HE SAID/SHE SAID WITHOUT BREAKS: I have derived a number of my "overuse" examples (not the exact words) from writing I have copyedited. I undertook one manuscript with great cheer, in the belief that the work was fairly clean and well polished. I was wrong! The past-tense verb "said" appeared on each page about five, six, or seven times. "Said" is reputed by many authors to be a silent verb, not noticed by the reader. That is the case in most instances, but not with so many repetitions. Then the word becomes like a burr under one's skin: annoying.

Any of dozens of other verbs can be chosen as a replacement for "said": stated, ranted, screamed, debated, considered, warned, exclaimed, explained, counseled, advised, threatened, pointed out, noted, commented, remarked, indicated, raved, cried, promised, begged, pleaded, dictated, shouted, commanded, and so on. In fiction, these verbs do not detract, but rather help by showing feeling, mood, and subtle connotations that fill in for our inability to hear tone of voice. Certainly, these, too, can be overused and should be sprinkled in with restraint, rather than with a liberal hand.

In addition to varying the he said/she said pattern, one can leave quotes without attribution if the speaker is not easily mistaken. In a two-person scene, in which one is male and one female, the identity of the one who says, *"I'm pregnant"*, can usually be deduced without much thought. Likewise for other facts that we know about one character versus the second, or even simply the mood of the one person versus the other in a scene.

However, beware. While a series of exchanges may remain unattributed, even *that* might create a pattern which can become wearisome and should be varied with attribution. The attribution here also prevents the reader from having to track the speaker over more than a couple of sentences.

Yet another means of variation from the he said/she said pattern is to indicate an action on the speaker's part so we know who has spoken without confusion or attribution. The movement or action also breaks up the dialogue which itself can become tedious without variation or interruption. The form in this instance would be: *"I wish I had more time to spend with you." He gazed into her eyes with great sincerity.* The action at this point, as well as the speech, will further denote character feeling, *"I wish I had more time to spend with you." He turned from her and gazed off into the dark night.* Perhaps in this case we already suspect he is lying to her, but his turning away might confirm our fear.

4. THE USE OF THE SAME DISTINCTIVE WORDS OR PARTS OF WORDS OR PHRASES: Don't write: *I disagreed with her, which turned into a major disagreement.* Why bother? You can say. *I disagreed with her, which turned into a major unpleasantness.*

You can go further than mere avoidance of exact-word repetition. Some words sound similar or have word parts that are similar. These should be avoided in near proximity, too. *I set down the book as she settled in her chair* can be changed to *I placed the book in front of her as she settled in her chair.* In my own writing, I just corrected the sentence: *Be aware of the possibility of error.* The repeated "r" sound was bothersome, so I changed *aware* to *cognizant.*

Words that rhyme are to be struck down immediately. *What she said was true. She didn't have a clue.* This can become: *What she said was accurate. She didn't have a clue.*

The wonderful fact is—you can nearly always find a substitute for the word that isn't quite right or sounds too much like another or that you've used before. Once in a while, no surrogate can be found, but this is rare. In such cases, you must grin and let it go for now. On the next draft, you might find a solution to the problem.

Admittedly, you won't always pick up each and every repetition on your first couple of go-throughs—or ever. The goal of variation in form and sound is a worthy one, but the end point is not always entirely achieved. Don't groan and fall to the floor when you find a failure in your published work. In fact, that's why many of us don't read our work again once it's in print.

Remember, certain phrases are genuinely invisible because they belong to the world in general, but sometimes a phrase that is all your own will alert the reader to a special turn of your very personal style. Take care with that and notice if you put the exact same, special wording into different characters' mouths. That's a no-no.*

---

*Here's a quote from a reader/author regarding phrase overuse: "Yes, definitely certain phrases get overused by authors. I remember reading one series where I was sure to find the protagonist 'speaking evenly,' 'saying evenly,' 'replying evenly,' or whatever, two or three times a book. And it stuck out.

"On the writer's side, I can attest that one doesn't always notice when one is doing that . . . in my books, folks are always grinning . . . I did a word search on a manuscript, and there were all those grins glaring at me. So that's probably what happened with . . . 'evenly'." Toni L. P. Kelner

5. THE USE OF THE SAME LENGTH WORDS: Even the number of syllables in words must be varied. I quoted an example elsewhere in which there was a yellow flame and a wooden match. The first time I rewrote the sentence, I changed it to a yellow flame and long match to vary the adjective syllable numbers.

That's getting a little bit down to the terrible nitty-gritty, which might make many a novice run in fear. But, truly, I only mention this in passing. Not that the matter is irrelevant, but this is the type of repetition that you will pick up eventually with your own inner ear. Your inner ear might not be perfect, however, whose is? An awareness that even the same length adjectives can begin to strike the reader as overly rhythmic can help you recognize the occasional awkwardness. Don't dwell on this one, please.

In fact, don't obsess over any of the problems on the above list. But do remain aware of possible repeats and try to break up any overuse of wording or structure.

Watch for patterns in the larger fabric of the novel as well: three-person scenes, all male-female scenes, too many seductions or murders or birth scenes, any pattern to your chapters (except for the basic ones that ought to be consistent, such as the number of pages per chapter, or ending each chapter with a surprise).

You might establish other types of too-regular formats that should be avoided because they lack sophistication and fluidity—types of characters, unlikely situations, etc. Keep your eyes open at all times.

If you should go on to become a best-selling novelist, then you can either repeat some of the tricks that have made up your success, or seek to vary your strategies from novel to novel. Finally, at that point, the choice will be all yours.

| Exercises: |

THIS WAY AND THAT WAY: Write a long sentence. Express the same meaning using different key words. Break the sentence in two. Now, reunite the sentence as a dependent and independent clause. (A dependent clause can't stand on its own. An independent clause can.)

SEARCHING: You probably already know what words you overuse, but have you done a search throughout a manuscript for these? How many times did you actually use that favorite word of yours? Replace three-quarters of these with a different word or phrase. If you don't know which words you overuse, try "just" and "look." Both are frequently overused. Also search on the "ing" to see if you've overused the gerund form.

GET THE DEAD OUT

We've discussed passive writing, but I'd like to zero in on that again. Let's attempt to eliminate passive formations in our work (not easy and not always attainable). For instance, try to change such structures as *I was working . . .* to *I worked.* This is sometimes possible and sometimes not. Have a go at it, however.

I quote an example from Thirteen Days: A Memoir of the Cuban Missile Crisis by Robert F. Kennedy: *The USSR's supplying of arms to Cuba was having a profound effect on the people of the United States . . .* This could have been changed to *The USSR's supplying of arms to Cuba profoundly affected . . .*

Kennedy was a master of the passive voice. (His above-cited book, however, is fascinating.) I'll give one more example: *An examination of photography . . . showed several other installations.* This could have been changed to *The photographs showed.* That experts examined the photographs goes without saying.

Often, a sentence must be turned around to avoid passivity, which is what I did in writing this very statement. I had begun, *To avoid passivity . . .*

Sentences certainly may appear in a unique and out-of-order fashion all the same, if the wording strikes your ear as more eloquent. Simply be positive that you understand what technical elements are involved and that your preference for the passive form doesn't arise from the fact that you are used to it.

Try wiping out passive forms. Avoid the "There is" and "It is" type of sentences as much as you can.

Along these lines, I suggest that you limit equivocation in your writing. *She had some fear that he would come before she was entirely ready* can become *She feared he would arrive before she was ready.*

Naturally, you can make exceptions to this suggested practice when you must explain that her fear was only partial.

The sense of your communication takes precedence over the wording. Alternatives to passive forms exist, though, and you can find them.

Literary Sludge

Passive and/or awkward construction is not uncommon. These forms exist in the "best" literature. Yikes! The following are from classic authors.

1. From "The Boarded Window" by Ambrose Bierce:

Many of them had already forsaken that region for the remoter settlements, but among those remaining was one who had been of those first arriving.

2. From "Araby" by James Joyce: *The wild garden behind the house contained a central apple-tree and a few straggling bushes, under one of which I found the late tenant's rusty bicycle-pump. He had been a very charitable priest; in his will he had left all his money to institutions and the furniture of his house to his sister.*

3. From "The Ambitious Guest" by Nathaniel Hawthorne: *For a moment it [the wind] saddened them, though there was nothing unusual in the tones. But the family were glad again when they perceived that the latch was lifted by some traveler, whose footsteps had been unheard amid the dreary blast which heralded his approach, and wailed as he was entering, and went moaning away from the door.*

4. From "The Girls in Their Summer Dresses" by Irwin Shaw: *Fifth Avenue was shining in the sun when they left the Brevoort and started walking toward Washington Square. The sun was warm, even though it was November, and everything looked like Sunday morning—the buses, and the well-dressed people walking slowly in couples and the quiet buildings with the windows closed.*

5. From "The Lottery" by Shirley Jackson, a story always reprinted as a best ever: *The morning of June 27th was clear and sunny, with the fresh warmth of a full-summer day; the flowers were blossoming profusely and the grass was richly green. The people of the village began to gather in the square, between the post office and the bank, around ten o'clock; in some towns there were so many people that the lottery took two days and had to be started on June 26th.*

But in this village, where there were only about three hundred people, the whole lottery took less than two hours, so it could begin at ten o'clock in the morning and still be through in time to allow the villagers to get home for noon dinner.

6. From "The Use of Force" by the famed poet/physician William Carlos Williams: *As it happens we had been having a number of cases of diphtheria in the school to which this child went during that month and we were all, quite apparently, thinking of that, though no one had as yet spoken of the thing.*

7. From "To Build a Fire" by Jack London: *Day had broken cold and gray, exceedingly cold and gray, when the man turned aside from the main Yukon trail and climbed the high earth-bank, where a dim and little traveled trail led eastward through the fat spruce timberland. It was a steep bank, and he paused for breath at the top, excusing the act to himself by looking at his watch. It was nine o'clock. There was no sun nor hint of sun, though there was not a cloud in the sky. It was a clear day, and yet there seemed an intangible pall over the face of things, a subtle gloom that made the day dark, and that was due to the absence of sun.*

How do I explain why these famous and revered writers had such significant writing faults? Possibly critics of the time rated several of these authors too highly and that opinion was then set in stone.

Tastes and styles have changed as well. Poe was maudlin and florid. He wrote run-on sentences galore. Yet Poe, although little read, is greatly beloved even today. Poe's life was dramatic and the delightful actor John Astin recently brought his works to the stage. In other words—go figure. Most magazines would not accept Poe stories these days. As for the Hawthorne phrasing—the clumsiness stuns me. I also explain the poor writing in the above by saying that these were lesser works and not so well edited.

Exercises:

BETTER THAN THE BEST: Patch the above sentences by the literati and see if you can outshine them in your own writing from this point on. Now you know that fame is not always the measure of true excellence.

No HELPER VERBS: The use of assisting verbs weakens strong sentences. Go through some of your writing and, where possible, remove the helper verbs, such as in "*was* walking." Okay, keep going and remove the rest. . . . Ah, that's a relief. Use the most economical form of the verb possible.

THE WRITER SINGS

A piece of advice experts always give writers is to "find your voice" or, sometimes it's phrased, "find your own voice." I don't actually think that particular suggestion is necessary. We do, automatically, write in nothing but. There's no way you will write in any voice except your own without radical and deliberate attempts to write like someone else. Writing in your own voice doesn't have to be a conscious decision. The way you write, like your fingerprints and genetic makeup, belong to you.

Don't worry about writing in your own voice. You already do that—even if your moods and, thus, styles differ from piece to piece.

On the other hand, you have a speaking voice that sometimes changes due to the whiskey you drink, cigarettes you smoke, or dairy that you eat which gives you mucus. Sometimes you have to let yourself heal from these effects for your own natural voice to return.

Clearing away bad writing habits and developing good ones will never damage the voice you possess. These steps allow you to claim a more functional, stronger, longer-lasting voice, just as training with a voice coach can assist a singer. You have a natural ability, a bent, that won't be harmed by removing some of your misconceptions or inabilities born of not enough practice.

In these last several pages, I've tried to give you a few ideas to work with. Carry on as you will. I hope I've helped you find some new insights into the mechanics of writing more clearly.

I also want you to know that rules can be broken in order to give way to a writer's unique concepts. Don't imagine that just because you haven't seen something done before that you can't try it. Feel free. Maybe you'll be the next one to sell a breakthrough mystery that's innovative and completely fresh.

But don't forget the markets entirely. Write to the market, if you can. Your chance of selling, if that's important to you (it is to me), will improve.

I've tried to give you a feel for writing clear and strong narrative because that's what the publishers look for today. That's the type of writing readers prefer as well. We don't very often read the old, convoluted styles anymore because we're not used to it. Florid, overblown work no longer suits our taste.

Another Word-Choice Factor—the Audience

When writing to sell, you can try to match other market parameters as well, down to vocabulary. You won't use words with content that isn't right for the audience—such as four-letter words. So, too, you should try to match the level of your word use to the reading skill of the audience. Don't write down to your readers, but be aware whether this is a general readership or a less educated one. Simpler words can substitute for complex ones without spoiling the meaning, if your readers are young adults or a less professional audience.

The opposite is true, as well. If you want to appeal to an intellectual elite, be sure your word use rings a bell with these readers. Grab the thesaurus (or specialty dictionaries in some instances) and find the language with impact for that group.

Words, naturally, don't always substitute one for the other even though they have a similar meaning. Words used in our highly complex language have nuance—shades and subtext that are known through a cultural transmission and won't always be revealed by the dictionary.

Be sensitive to the nuance of words in addition to each one's simple, surface meaning. If words you don't know pop up in a book you read, or if you don't understand the fine distinction between that and another word, seek out the subtleties by asking friends in a writers' group, editing group online, or in the real world.

Continue to study the language—the writer's primary tool. Remain curious about how other writers use words. Browse in bookstores and dip into mysteries in the same subgenre in which you write. Look at reference works for authors—there are tons. Many books on word use also exist. Forage there. Words are your medium. Examine them as a painter scrutinizes new shades of paint or style of paintbrush.

Exercise:

LET'S HEAR YOUR VOICE: In order to prove to you how singular your own voice is, write paragraphs about the following. I can bet one thing: Your writing will be very, very different from anyone else's.

The situation is:

-Boy meets girl in the bookstore.

-A time of family crisis.

-The announcement of a pregnancy.

-A death.

This is a short exercise and won't take you much time. Try to follow some of the ideas we have discussed. Although you will have no one else's work to compare this to, I think that you'll be able to see that no other writer would have taken the path in these paragraphs that you have.

SUIT THE AUDIENCE: Write a paragraph. Re-write the same paragraph for a group of sixth graders. Re-write the paragraph for a professional group.

TIME OFF FOR SELF-EDITING

You can prepare your manuscript for submission in two ways: Hire an editor, which is an increasingly popular means of cleaning up a novel for potential sale, or, alternately, self-edit your copy, a much less-expensive proposition.

Although I'm a book doctor/editor myself, I have to advise you to choose the second means of smoothing out your own rough prose. You're the writer and if you intend to go on writing, to write more than one book and make more than one submission (in fact, to build a career for yourself), you should work out the literary kinks on your own. You'll learn a great deal from the process—which itself is one part of the general job description of "author."

My suggestion is to set your writing aside for at least a day or two before picking up the work again for editing. The purpose of the time lapse is to give you a new perspective on what you've written, so that you may have some objectivity. Usually, though, if you have written a whole novel, you haven't seen your early chapters for a few weeks at a minimum.

Be Bloody, Bold, and Resolute

Being in love with your own words, your own creation, is a very early stage of authorship. Words are lovely creatures and strung together in certain harmonious ways can be very, very pleasing. In fact, that is what we have been working on in this section—the assembling of language to form exciting sentences. However, contrarily, words are cheap. There are more of them where these came from. You have put a vast mass of words into electronic bits in order to shape them to a maximally, satisfying form. Cut the dross.

Self-editing requires that you be objective about your work, so that you may serve as your own editor. Don't cling to the words you have already written unless they are perfect. If they aren't, discard them with ruthless abandon. That's the self-editing activity. You are now polishing as a real craftsperson or artist does. If you need to chuck whole paragraphs into oblivion for the greater good of the overall novel, do so. You may save scraps in separate files if you think you can make something of them later on—a short story perhaps—but cut the words, sentences, paragraphs from the main body of the novel if they don't fit.

Do not allow yourself to be self-indulgent. Both editors and readers will be able to tell, exactly as you can, that these parts do not belong in the text. What do you care about more strongly—your precious few words or your reputation for clean and professionally written narrative?

Editing is not a one-step affair because flaws, however subtle, abound in a work. Every "draft" or go-through of the manuscript will reveal further needed changes, with probably no end in sight. Each subsequent time you review the written work, additional errors have been cleared away, leaving other aspects exposed to scrutiny.

This is why more than one pass is needed.

Moreover, with each change, you should re-read the sentence that you have altered, and sometimes the sentences before and after that one as well. Each adjustment of wording transforms meaning and rhythm, mandating other tailoring to suit the corrections. Such is the process.

The more literary your work, the more you will need to perfect your words. That's the job. No one said writing is easy. The time and skills required are an awesome burden. The immediate rewards can be minimal. But what else did you have in mind to do with your life?

How many drafts, then, must you go through? Personally, I only do three for most of my fiction. However, I have brought more and more factors into my conscious mind that I am able to be cognizant of within my very first draft.

Also, that three-draft rule is not true for all of my work. The more word-bound the project, the more polishing I do. I probably did about nine drafts for each chapter of *Pacific Empire* because the language was so important in that novel. Additionally, even within that nine-draft scope, I went over many sentences a generous multiple of that nine times. (Nonfiction, I draft only twice—well, maybe three times.)

The Sound Is Key

How is copyediting actually performed? I sit at the word processor and read the sentences inside my head. To do that requires greater quiet than does the initial setting down in words, because I have to hear the rhythm as well as everything else. Some authors say, for this, they read their work out loud so they can actually hear it with their ears. If that's what it takes for them—or you—fine. Be sure, either way, that you do take into account the rhythm of the sentences. What does rhythm mean in writing? I've never heard appropriate rhythm defined, yet this does have to do with how the words and sentences sound to the inner ear.

If you feel your inner ear is poor, ask a friend to read over the manuscript for you. But this is a big job, one requiring skill, and few can do it. Often your friend might be too polite to be critical, or you become too defensive in hearing the results to benefit from the help. Don't forget, either, if you rely on a pal to read over the story or novel, you owe that person a similar favor. This is a large undertaking for which a professional editor will charge big dollars . . . At least appreciate what you've asked your buddy to do.

How do you know when you're done copyediting your work? Generally, you are finished at the point at which you have very few substantial corrections. This doesn't mean the work is flawless. Writing is never, ever, quite exactly perfect. If, a few months later, you pick up anything you've written, you'll see the changes you ought to have made. But our society is a fast-paced one and we don't have the luxury—and who really has the desire?—to rehash a project year after year, after the writing is essentially complete.

Being fastidious and perfectionistic is nice—up to a point. Once that point has been reached, don't go on with the editing. Authors can begin to pick their prose to bits in obsessive and unproductive ways. Sooner or later, the self-editing process has to stop and the writing has to go into the mail, or email, to the agent or to the editor.

Trust me completely when I say that person's acceptance of your novel will not depend on a few words here or there. While the manuscript must be publishable as is, a few nit-picky details don't matter at all. The impact of the work is what will count. Have you written a good story here, an interesting and absorbing one? If so, you will find a publisher, even if the first submission (or first ten) bounces back to you.

In the meantime, while waiting to hear, begin your next mystery. Nothing takes the pressure off so much as a brand new focus that will keep you entertained. Go on.

Exercises:

OVER AND OVER AND OVER AGAIN: Take a few pages of your book and go through, making corrections until you think the piece is nearly perfect. Set this aside for a week. Now, look again. Do further errors come to light? They usually do. Correct these and set aside for another week. The gremlins get in there; shoo them away.

RHYTHM . . . AND BLUES: Take those same pages—or others, if you're sick of these—and read out loud to yourself. Listen for sentences that run too long, for words that clash with other words, and for phrases that sound "all wrong." Now fix the writing. *Always* read for the sound.

6

After
the
Fact

—————————— **THE AUTHOR'S SUMMATION** ——————————

Into every life, a little rain must fall. Writing the summary for your mystery is not a pleasant task (does anyone enjoy this?) but it is a necessary one if you expect to submit for publication—or merely, to begin with, to agents.

Here are a few tips.

I write my novels as individual chapters so that when I revise I can do so in discrete chunks. In writing the summary you can either put the whole novel together in one document or call up each chapter as you go. You will need to look at all your work again to bring back to mind what happens in the chapters. You might think that you will remember everything—you wrote the darn book, after all—but you won't. You didn't write the mystery overnight; you have been at it at least a couple of months and memory sometimes fades, especially as to sequence of events.

Certainly you can summarize each chapter as you write it, tucking your notes into a file exclusively for that, but usually your focus at that point is elsewhere. Don't try to divide your attention too much during the actual writing process.

How long should your summary of each chapter be? As long as it takes to include the major events. You will go back a few times and refine your summary, so right now the writing of the first draft doesn't matter all that much. The length of your coverage for each chapter also depends on how many chapters your mystery contains. Obviously a summary of a 4,000-word chapter with 14 to the book will be a different length than the summary of a 1,500-word chapter.

At any rate, the summary of a chapter should only require a few sentences that will comprise one paragraph, or two at the most. The overall, final length of your summary will be anywhere from three to seven or eight single-spaced pages. And are they single-spaced? That might depend on the requirement of the particular publisher. Some ask for summaries to be double-spaced, but mine are single-spaced, as per my agent.

A general rule for summaries is that shorter is better. Once you have gathered all your paragraphs summarizing the chapters, you can begin to refine the total document and to slenderize it. The summary may be very important in the sale of your book. Or it might make zero difference in the end. That depends on the editor and how he/she likes to approach a mystery novel. Some editors will review the summary and a few pages of the actual writing. Some don't care to examine a summary at all. Since you don't know which type of editor you are submitting to, you will have to make the summary as enticing as possible. Enticing means readable. Readable means short and to the point. The summary, which is written in present tense, isn't supposed to typify your style, just give the highlights of the plot. Start smoothing out your language and deleting extraneous details. This is the skeleton—the bones bare of all flesh.

However lean the summary might be, make it interesting. Stress the most dramatic moments of your novel. Highlight the conflict. Let the impact of the mystery you have written come though here. Include the solution/conclusion to your story. The editor wants to see if the upshot is worth the development.

Go through that summary even more times than you have gone through the novel itself. This piece of work must stand on its own. Let it read as a standalone story of a sort. Show the action vividly, but sparingly, without introducing too many secondary characters. You don't have the room.

Done? Go through once again and tighten—and heighten—the summary.

Exercises:

IN AS FEW WORDS AS POSSIBLE: If you have outlined a story or novel, take that and turn the piece into a summary, making a readable narrative. Set this aside for a couple of weeks. Go back and read what you have. Can you follow the action as a reader—not the author?

SHORTER STILL: Done with your summary? Bravo, congrats. Now and cut out another 20 percent. Can't be done? Yes, it can. You have left in material you don't at all need.

THE HIRED GUN

Not all agents belong to the Association of Authors Representatives (AAR), an organization that requires them to stipulate to an ethical code of conduct, but which also rakes in heavy dues from its members. Just because an agent you're interested in doesn't belong, doesn't mean he/she is unethical. The agent any new author is most likely to sign with may likely be an independent agent, who might not have the bucks to sign up with AAR. So don't let that detail throw you off. But DO inquire around as to the agent's reputation. There are places on the Internet—such as the site Predators and Editors <http://www.sfwa.org/prededitors/>—that discuss the agents who have done someone dirty, so check out these sites, but also ask on any of the digests or listservs you receive.

For those trying to obtain information on particular agents' reputations and who aren't online, I was going to advise you to call Mystery Writers of America, but then I realized that the administrative director might simply refer you to me . . . Well, the blunt truth is that today being wired (online) is the fastest and best way to receive up-to-date information, so I'd suggest signing on.

What you will hear from most new mystery writers, actually, is a discouraging tale about trying to snag themselves an agent. This is no exaggeration. Agents are tough to come by and, as the mainstream downscales mysteries, getting tougher. Any one agent can only serve so many clients in a halfway decent manner, while some, believe it or not, don't even have an interest in mystery—unless you're James Lee Burke or Steve Martini.

So how are you going to acquire an agent? Again, ask around. But please don't be rude. No inquiry is so indelicate as: "Who's your agent? ". No one you know thinks your writing is worth being represented by the agent who represents him or her, so forget it. You can ask, "Do you know of any agents who represent mystery and who might be taking on new clients? ". And, by the way, this is one reason we network and join mystery writers groups specifically. Your old friend from the neighborhood won't have an answer to that question.

Another source of agents is AAR, naturally, which maintains an online site <http://www.publishersweekly .com/aar/>. AAR charges to mail you its list, if you're not online, but a list is somewhat useless without specific agent guidelines. A better source of agent listings is the *Literary Market Place*, a copy of which is in your local library's reference section (ask the librarian). One good bet is to look in

Publishers Weekly in the Hot Deals column and also in the Forecasts section and see who the agents selling mysteries are.

All types of other reference books promise agent listings, so sit in Barnes & Noble and take a few notes. You're better off not buying these, actually. Pick one or two agents from each of the reference works and see if you even get a courteous reply. These agents might be inundated from other readers of the same volumes.

Many (even most) agents have an assistant in the office whose job it is to open your envelope. He or she scans your cover letter for two or three indicators signaling that you might be worthy of being a client. If you don't have a track record or an outstanding career in another field, your beautiful material might go right in the trash. In its place, you will find your self-addressed, stamped envelope (SASE) filled with a 10th-generation-copy reject letter and an ad for the agent's book on how to sell your blockbuster mystery.

The above information might not sound helpful, but you have to understand that there is nothing easy about getting an agent—or, in fact, anything in this profession. You have to work at making progress step by step, year by year, with many a setback. Just keep plugging. The only thing worse than failing to achieve your dream is never having one—or never taking a risk to reach for the vision with which you've been gifted.

Direct to the Slushpile?

Many writers ask if they really need an agent. The answer is that you are better off having an agent in order to sell a book (definitely with the largest publishers), but sometimes getting an agent is so impossible that it's best to go ahead and query the publishers directly. First, however, find out which publishers will have a look at unagented material. Many will, but some absolutely won't.

Also, the best approach is to check with the publisher by phone for a contact name, even if you have a reference book with editors listed in it. The publishing business changes so quickly that by this time next week, three editors will be at different houses than they were today. I'm exaggerating, but only very slightly. Many editors who have become identified with a certain publisher have been there forever and will stay until retirement, perhaps. Nonetheless, it pays to double-check—and to be sure that the editor will accept unagented submissions. The expense of printing and mailing a query is much greater than the cost of a quick telephone call to New York.

Once you've signed a contract with an agent, after months of searching, what should you expect from your new authors' rep? Honestly, don't expect a really big push. This will be a bitter disappointment to many and will cause a lot of complaint on the part of naïve clients, but, at the start, an agent is not going to do that much to make you happy. He or she will send around a few copies of your manuscript. And then will forget about you.

However, that's better than the situation for a couple of mystery authors I know whose agents were the really, really, old-fashioned kind. These reps sent out one solitary offering and waited some months to receive a manuscript rejection before mailing off a second submission of the book. The authors liked their agents personally, but that type of inaction is somewhat ridiculous. Multiple submissions by agents are the rule today and one thing you have a right to expect.

Beyond that, you can expect to hear about the rejections as they come in—even have copies of the rejection letters sent to you periodically. Once in a great while, you can call the agent and expect a telephone conversation. That's about it. Although you have paid with blood, sweat, and tears, you haven't paid with money to date, so don't really anticipate that much more service. If you feel your agent isn't doing enough for you, you can leave, but often the next one you find—if you find one—isn't significantly better.

My advice is that it's counterproductive to criticize your agent to his or her face. Yes, your agent is slow—it's a trait of the profession—plus you aren't his or her only client. Yes, the agent could have submitted to several other publishers, but he/she didn't feel that the response on the manuscript to date warranted the effort.

And, certainly, your agent will take 15 percent of any money you earn from the book. Now that amount might be nothing. Or it might be a few thousand dollars, that's all. Better understand right off that the agent isn't always going to spend a few hundred of his/her own money in time and postage for the promise of such a minimal return. Don't whine. Just work harder to make yourself a more attractive and viable client.

Your agent, for that reason, continues to be your market number one. If anything good happens in regard to your writing, publicize that fact to your agent by sending a note. Your agent is the primary person who needs to think your work is sensational. Make sure he/she understands your potential— not by calling and complaining, but by showing some real accomplishments such as getting published in a small press mystery magazine or being invited to talk to a group. Let your agent see that your writing rings bells. He or she will then work harder to get your mystery to the publishing houses.

SUBMITTING THE PACKAGE

Authors with agents won't have to go much further with their packages than the summary, unless the agent requests certain other material, such as a character list and bio. The agents will submit an entire manuscript to the publisher.

Charges for copying to reproduce the packages, and so on, will usually be deducted from the author's part of the sale advance. Some agencies charge these fees up front—not the same as a reading fee or other such, which should never be paid. Fees for phone calls, copying, and so on are considered fair. Personally, I don't think you should pay these fees prior to selling the mystery, but some new authors do this, and legitimately . . . Be very watchful of agent charges that come before a sale, however. Ask for an itemization, in fact.

For the author without an agent, a package should consist of a cover letter, previous reviews, the summary, and ancillary material such as a character list and a bio, and two or three chapters of the actual book. This is called a "partial," which should be used as an initial submission, unless the publisher states distinctly that it only wants query letters, not submissions. (This is how some of the romance lines handle it.) A submission solely by query letter makes your job very, very tough as you are sending nothing but a single page to represent your book. That letter had better be darn good.

Cover letters in any case are extremely important. Keep in

mind, first, that they are business letters and that you already have a summary of your work on hand, either to be sent now or later on. The cover letter coveys the mystery's "hook" and gives an overview in a mere two or three sentences. This page is, in essence, a marketing tool—both for your own marketing and from which a publisher may perhaps extract ideas later on. The best thing I can do is to give you a sample:

Dear Editor:

Pie in the Sky *heroine Helen Robbins drinks Radegrst beer and reads Soldier of Fortune magazine while hunting the revolutionaries who have skyjacked at least five executive jets.*

The first of a series, Pie in the Sky *is an 86,000-word adventure/mystery that follows the feisty Ms. Robbins to Mexico and beyond, as she investigates for the Private Plane Pilots Association.*

A long-time pilot myself, I have, in writing this book, used what I know about the vulnerabilities of civil aviation today. My previous nonfiction articles about the small-jet industry have appeared in national publications such as Flying *and* Airplane Owners Weekly. *Two of my short mysteries were published in* Death By Murder, *an anthology put out by* Helter Skelter Magazine.

Pie in the Sky, *which includes romance, intrigue, and both domestic and international settings, is entirely finished and ready to be reviewed. I hope this novel will suit your imprint and I have enclosed a stamped, self-addressed envelope for your response.*

I look forward to hearing from you and thank you in advance for your time.

Very truly yours,

In other words, the query/cover letter is the pitch and isn't detailed at all. It also doesn't resemble your writing.

In both the query and the partial, you can include copies of reviews of any other work of yours or even a copy of a featured interview with you as an author—or, in the above case, pilot. If the interview is long, however, you can include the first page only or part of the first couple of columns, a jump line (continued on page x), and the conclusion in a cut-and-paste that takes up only one page. Some material, such as a long review, can be photocopied onto the front and back of a single sheet.

Similarly, for a package that includes chapters, you can insert a bio page, if that is of some consequence. The bio should show your background credentials: "As a certified flight instructor, I have also appeared at FAA events representing my flight school." Despite the fact that this is not a writing credit, the item does establish your ability to appear in public and promote.

Use your judgment, but never forget that any supporting material should be brief, punchy, and to the point. The editor is merely going to breeze through your submission. Appealing pages and luck will win you the opportunity to send the entire manuscript.

Exercise:

FIND THE HOOK: Find the one line that expresses the conflict in your novel best. That's your hook for your query. For example: Can an 80-year old, one-legged ex-cop stop a homicidal maniac from killing again? (Woah, we hope so.) That might even be the first line of your letter. But from there be businesslike and not too clever.

——————— TAKING OUT A CONTRACT ———————

I need to say just a few things about contracts because, should you get to this point, with or without an agent, you have to be somewhat alert.

Often, the editor will call at home to inform you that the publisher wants to take on your book, a stunning moment. (Also be aware of this in setting your call-blocking options— here is a call from an unknown number that you might want.) As emotional as you will be when the phone call comes, tell yourself right now that you will not burble any agreements in the heat of the moment. You might be agreeing to something—making a contract, that is—with adverse consequences.

"Of course I'll let you publish my novel *Undue Books* for $300 and 1 percent royalties, all rights included." I don't think so.

Right at this second, when you've heard the fabulous news of your novel's acceptance, your hearing might not be too good nor your thinking too clear. Practice saying, "I'm extremely flattered. I'll have to consider that and let you know." Be pleasant but don't be pushed into acceding to anything.

After you hang up, call your agent.

No agent? After you hang up, call a friend who has an agent and get the agent's number, or be ready with the name and number of an agent you would like to sign with. Prepare a couple of names and telephone listings, in fact. Although with the promise of a contract you'll certainly be able to get someone to represent you, you might not get the agent who works for Mary Higgins Clark.

If the offer is from a small press and you don't feel you need or want an agent for the deal, the above advice about not speaking up right away still holds true. Don't agree to any specifics until you see the offer in print. I'm not against an author looking over a contract with a small press him or herself, but consider a couple of issues first:

• How long does the contract give the publisher to bring out the book? The time frame should be reasonable—say 18 months.

• Do you get an advance against royalties? Royalties are the author's pay, most often calculated as a percent of the book's cover price, but sometimes figured in different ways—especially by the smaller presses. An advance against royalties is yours to keep, even if the books don't sell. However, to make additional earnings after an advance, the book has to sell more than the number that would account for the advance payment. Often, the advance, if there is one, is the only money an author will ever see.

• What are the royalty percents? Are they a standard 6, 7, or 8 percent? Are they at least 35 percent for an e-book? What about for print on demand books, which are not such a great initial investment for the publisher? Print on demand books are printed one at a time using special presses and an electronic file. Ten percent might be offered, but would a higher figure be more equitable? (I've heard as high as 50 percent on POD, but only to name authors.)

• Who owns the ancillary (also called secondary or subsidiary) rights? The more of these rights—covering sale to book clubs, sale to film studios, audio book sales, and much more—that you get to keep, the better. If little or no advance is paid, you should get a higher percentage of the additional rights. At the same time, publishers are now trying to grab a greater percentage of this potential for profit. Watch out here.

• When does the book go out of print and when do all rights revert back to you? That's another question that is more and more germane, due to the technology that allows publishers to say a book is "in print" simply because books can be quickly ordered from an existing file. Most e-book contracts set a timeframe for one year, after which the contract may be discussed again.

Be aware that even small press publishers will negotiate. You don't have to give in to everything they want. Even if this is their standard contract, the publisher will accept a change or two.

If all the above seems too complex, try again to find that agent by word of mouth. An agent with whom someone else is satisfied is your best shot. Finding an agent when you have a contract in hand is a lot easier than when you're starting out green.

JOINING A GANG

One of the best things that a writer can do, aside from sticking his/her butt to the chair and pounding the keyboard, is to join one or more writers' societies for moral support, market information, and as a means of networking. Luckily for those of us who write—or want to write—mysteries, a number of very active groups in this arena exist both in the real world and on the Net.

If you don't know these organizations yet, or have heard of them but don't know how to link yourself up, here are the details.

Mystery Writers of America is the leading association for professional mystery writers. Members of MWA include a large percentage of the major, published mystery authors, as well as screenwriters, dramatists, new-media writers, editors, publishers, and other professionals in the mystery field.

Several categories of membership have been designated and anyone interested in writing mystery fiction will fit into one. MWA is a very active group that sends monthly newsletters and sponsors the Edgar Awards given at a yearly banquet in New York City. Regional MWA chapters undertake many activities, including dinner meetings, and have their own newsletters as well. Check out MWA at <http://www.mysterywriters.net/> or write to Mary Beth Becker, Administrative Director, Mystery Writers of America, 17 E. 47th St., 6th floor, NYC, NY 10017; 212/888-8171. (You can reach her through the website, too.) She'll send you a membership application.

The organization called Sisters in Crime (SinC) fashioned itself "to combat discrimination against women in the mystery field, educate publishers and the general public as to inequities in the treatment of female authors, raise awareness of their contribution to the field, and promote the professional advancement of women who write mysteries." SinC is now more than a decade old and has a membership of well over three thousand worldwide, with more than 50 chapters in the U.S., Canada, and Hamburg, Germany. There are many "brothers" in the group, as well as sisters.

SinC's on-going projects include a Books in Print catalog that lists members' work and which goes out twice a year to 10,000-plus wholesalers, distributors, libraries, bookstore chains, mystery bookstores, and other independent bookstores. SinC supports special interest groups for authors of color, writers of true crime, writers of young adult and juvenile mysteries, and prepublished writers.

The organization maintains booths at the American Library Association National Convention, as well as at regional conventions and regional American Booksellers Association Trade Shows. Group ads are taken in *Publishers Weekly* once a year for the magazine's survey of the mystery genre. Membership in SinC is really a good step for a budding mystery author to take. Once you have joined the parent organization, you can then join a chapter in your geographic area.

Contact Executive Director, Beth Wasson at P.O. Box 442124, Lawrence, KS 66044-8933, by e-mail at: sistersincrime@juno.com, by telephone at 785/842-1325, or by fax at 785/842-1034.

Cybergroups Rule

The Internet organizations circulate digests on a daily basis and will key you in to what is going on in the world of mystery. Members can answer almost any question you have about agents, editors, manuscript presentation, and other current industry details. These digests also provide a forum for you to present yourself. You can blatantly promote here when you have a book or a story coming out or create a presence even before that actually happens.

Authors might well want to try the very active daily list provided by the SinC Internet Chapter, which has a site at

<http://www.sinc-ic.org/>. To subscribe to sinc-ic-digest, send the following message to majordomo@angus.mystery.com: "subscribe sinc-ic-digest". Happily, the list is a short one and usually can be read in situ, without your having to download a file for later consumption.

Also short is the daily chat of a group whose members tell you to ask them about their briefs. This is the Short Mystery Fiction Society, a mostly writers group that boasts authors who actively sell their work to the main mystery magazines. Stick around because as new markets emerge, you'll hear it here first. Founded by Deadly Alibi Press honcho Margo Power, SMFS declares as its intention "to actively recognize writers and readers who promote and support the creative art form of short mysteries." To that end, the group has created the short mystery story Derringer awards, which has garnered growing recognition. SMFS is a friendly group of a comfortable size. To subscribe, send an email message to Shortmystery-subscribe@onelist.com.

SMFS publishes a netletter called The Short Order, issues of which can be found at <http://www.thewindjammer.com /smfs/html/newsletter.html>.

The most famous mystery group on the Internet is the three-thousand-member DorothyL. This nearly ten-year-old list includes just-plain readers and authors galore and is, for the most part, a welcoming place. Take a while though before posting any initial notes; Dlers can be a touchy lot and being flamed by these mystery lovers isn't much fun. (But don't let that warning put you off. DL is an important place for mystery writers and will soon become a complete addiction.)

The mission statement of DorothyL tells us that it is "a

discussion and idea list for the lovers of the mystery genre."
The group is named in honor of one of the great women
mystery writers of the last century, Dorothy L. Sayers. To subscribe to DorothyL, send an email message to
LISTSERV@LISTSERV.KENT.EDU and write only "subscribe
DorothyL your name" You will receive a message back asking
you to confirm your subscription in order to verify your
address. The kindly listowners who keep the members in rel-
ative order are Kara L. Robinson and Diane Kovacs—both
librarians. The daily digest regularly runs from 30 to 80 mes-
sages and is sometimes a download in text.

A new group adding members day by day is Wicked
Company, an iUniverse community of mystery writers,
chaired by wit and author D. L. Browne. You don't have to
have a book contracted with print-on-demand publisher
iUniverse to become a member. Just sign in and sign up at
<http://communities.iuniverse.com/mystery101>. Then
sign on to the email group. You won't be sorry. Ms. Browne
is a very proper hostess.

If there's not a group here to suit your circumstances, try
to find one at the Deadly Directory/Cluelass site
<http://www.cluelass.com> run by Kate Derie. Derie, in
fact, was awarded a special Derringer Reader Award for
Significant Contribution in Support of the Short Story by
SMFS in 1999. Her site is useful for many additional purposes,
such as finding publications and publishers.

Derie has herself started a list for authors trying to promote their mysteries, called Murder Must Advertise. Join the
group and learn about promotion. Here's how you get there:
<http://www.onelist.com/community/MurderMustAdvertise>.

How about getting in touch with the Historical Mystery

Appreciation Society, which puts out a newsletter for about $17 or so a year for three big issues? The web site is at <http://www.themysterybox.com/hmas>. Or go and read HMAS founder Sue Feder's "Magical Mystery Tour Reviews." The web site is <http://members.home.net/monkshould>.

TAKING THE RAP

Whole books are written about promotion, so I'll just touch on a few factors that will help, if and when you get to the point of needing this information.

People feel comfortable doing different things in order to promote. Some individuals might be terrific presenters, and authors who are ought to drum up opportunities for presentations. As a writer, I've always felt most comfortable writing pieces for various magazines and newsletters to promote my name. Many fiction authors don't feel they can write non-fiction, so they ought not.

Can you call a store and pitch a signing? That's hard for me, but if you can do it, go right ahead. Can you do radio interviews? Give flyers to cab drivers and anyone else who comes your way? These are all good avenues for marketing your published novel.

If you're not someone who can make any of these efforts, do you have a little bit of money for postcards or ads, or pens and magnets imprinted with the name of your book?

What is your particular approach, something that you can do to stimulate interest in your mystery?

The main idea is that you must do something. The publishers themselves are known to do very little nowadays and the responsibility falls upon the author. The general standard is that the mystery publishers will send galleys to a few of the mystery reviewers at *Publishers Weekly*, *Kirkus* (which is known to write poor reviews of most mysteries), *Library Journal*, *Booklist*, Marilyn Stasio at *The New York Times*, and a few other places.

Reviews are important, especially from these sources, as any mention of a mystery, much less a rave, encourages the book-stores and libraries to order the book. Reviews can also go into any promotion package you yourself put together in trying to obtain further reviews, signings, and speaking engagements.

I recommend that you do make up a nice little package for yourself, well before your book comes out. Include such materials as any pre-reviews or blurbs for the book, a fact sheet explaining who the author is, and something of the background of the mystery. Write an interview of yourself, if you are able, and note in the press kit that any publication wanting to pick it up, in whole or in part, may.

Make the package as special as you can: Use a color paper that coordinates with the cover of the book. Photocopy the cover in color if you don't have actual jackets and include that. Include an author's photo if you think that will help. Whatever you can do to add pizzazz without being mean-ingless or overly showy, do it. You don't have to send trinkets that will head immediately for the trashcan, such as a rubber knife or plastic gun, but do try to catch the eye of someone opening the promotion piece and make the information you include substantive.

Author promotion is an ongoing process. If you are lucky enough to have a book come out in print, or even an elec-tronic book, market your heart out. This is your opportunity.

You've worked hard to write the novel and get it published. Now make the most of it.

Hire a Publicist?

Should you hire an outside publicist? That's very expensive, but some people do. When I say very expensive, I mean you have to approach a publicist well prior to the publication of your book and often fork over thousands of dollars as a retainer. Can the publicist help? Yes and no. The person you have hired will try (ask for details of her activity). If her contacts are good and your background is marketable, she might be able to get you interviews or spots on radio, television, or in print. If you have a less impressive background and little expertise, the sell will be a harder one with fewer results. If you're a go-getter, you can do your own publicity, often with an exciting outcome.

What works in publicity? That's a question every published author asks with very few answers. No one actually knows which selling approaches or public appearances will turn the tide. The truth is you just have to keep right on pitching. Sooner or later, someone will say, "I've heard your name, haven't I? I just don't know where." That's actually a good sign, very good. Even if they don't recall the title of the book you've been pounding the pavement and the keyboard over for months, they know your name.

Or maybe they think you are some other author. Oh well. Keep up those marketing efforts anyway.

Promotion Tip: Giving an Interview

I've been on both sides of the interview equation and having first stood in the role of the interviewer, I know that what the journalist generally wants is simple: answers. If you are eager to promote yourself, keep in mind the basic fact that being as forthcoming as possible will earn you more print space or media time than being tightlipped.

Recently, I was sent an ARC (advanced reading copy) of a Famous Person's latest novel. An invitation to interview her came along with the book, and, as a review plus an interview is a format I often choose for my subjects, I followed up on that. The woman's publicist gave me her fax number so I could conduct a question and answer session. I faxed the FP a few questions based on my reading of about 30 pages.

The responses were, sorry to say, unusable. Why? They were mere scraps of replies and didn't say much. There was little I could do to dress the material in a way that was sufficient to provide my readers with an article.

How could the FP have done a better job so that her time and mine wouldn't have been wasted? Or in other words, how can you handle an interview in the best possible manner? To maximize the possibility of your material being used, you can answer the questions that both are and aren't being asked.

Part of the FP's novel is set in New Mexico, which led me to ask a question about the state, which she then said she had no knowledge of. That left a dead end and a dead space in my potential interview. Suppose she had said, instead, "I don't know X, but I know Y, which is what prompted me to include that particular background in my novel. Having seen Y, I felt passionately about it and wanted to elicit a similar passion in my readers."

If she had gone into topic Y at any length at all, I could

have reconstructed my question easily and used her response.

The same holds true for interviews that require you to speak extemporaneously. I was recently invited to discuss a topic on National Public Radio, and went to the studio to record my comments. The reporter doing the story in this case didn't really know what questions to ask.

I have been there, believe me, having written many, many stories on topics I knew nothing about. His hemming and hawing was an invitation to me to head in whatever direction my thoughts would take me. I jumped in at each of his hesitations. Instead of spending 15 minutes taping this, as the reporter expected, we spent half an hour, giving me a greater opportunity to provide him with the material he could use in editing his piece—and a better chance to get in some promotion for myself.

In talking to a reporter or providing written answers for an article on your mystery, never hold back. The biggest mistake you can make is to say too little. Too many words can always be cut down and edited; too few words can rarely be puffed up to create a credible profile for publication. Your object in giving an interview is to promote yourself, and your work. Go ahead and do just that.

I kept FP's name on my list for a few days, hoping that I could make something of the statements she had sent me. In the end, I reviewed her answers once again and found them completely insubstantial.

I crossed FP's name from my list of projects to complete. There are enough FPs or potential FPs out there who will add the dash of effort that a vivid and fun interview requires. Seize the moment. Even more than FP, new authors must make every opportunity count.

—————— Private Security Detail ——————

You don't have to worry too much about your intellectual property being stolen, at least not by agents and editors. That's rare. However, what some alleged agents, so-called publishers, and fraudulent editorial setups do want is your money. Don't give it to them. I'm a firm believer in not handing over dollars to anyone for anything, unless it can't be helped, such as with the IRS.

Don't pay to be represented and don't pay to be published. Ever. Never agree to a reading fee. These are scams. Some agencies known to represent clients in a legitimate way also have an arm that charges newcomers for a manuscript review. Naïve authors imagine that simply because an agent represents Joe Mystery Star this is their big opportunity, if they include a check. The only chance being handed out here is the potential for coughing up their money for no consideration at all.

While freelance editors will charge for a manuscript evaluation, that's a different story, entirely. Their business is in dealing with client manuscripts on an upfront basis. With the agencies that ask for fees, and even publishers that do, their intention is to merely rip you off by misrepresenting the possibility of being published with them or through them.

Be careful, too, in signing with an agent once you've picked one. I know of an author who wants to get rid of her agent, but has found hardly a loophole in the contract to do so. That's not right. Most contracts with agents allow either party to withdraw upon notice—it's that simple. You have to be able to get out and move on.

Other opportunistic con artists put on a freelance editor's outfit, while promising to prune your prose. All they wind up trimming, however, is your pocketbook. I can't tell you who is good or who will be fair as a freelance editor. I can only say be careful out there. Don't allow the book doctors and editors to take advantage of your heartfelt desire to write for publication. If you're seeking someone to edit your work, ask for client references, or credentials, at the least (and don't accept all credentials at face value). You may also request a few paragraphs of sample edit to see if you will be paying for value and if your ideas are in accord with the editor's.

Irksome, mean-spirited, harmful scams abound in the world of the writer—agents who steer clients to a publishing contract not to their advantage and costly vanity presses like the notorious Commonwealth, which never issued paid-for books. Do not leap before checking into the deal you think will lead you to glory. Join a writers organization and query the group if some question comes up. You don't have to be preyed upon. Be savvy. Protect your interests.

KEEPING A SERIES ALIVE

Publishers are definitely still buying series books. First contracts are for one or two books and contracts thereafter can be for two or three. If a series sells well, the publisher will hope to keep you writing those novels and you will want to do so, too. What helps a series retain its freshness? How can you build in the elements that will keep up your interest, as well as the reader's?

Just as a short story has a short arc and limited scenes and settings and the novel has a wider arc, so the series has an even larger scope with its own ongoing tension and conflicts.

These forward driving series' conflicts are either (1) of the Sherlock Holmes/Moriarity type—that is, a continuing hero/villain struggle that is not truly finished at the end of a single volume; (2) a relationship dispute of some kind, such as between male/female, police officer/superior, or competitors such as prosecutor/defense attorney; or (3) an internal conflict, for example, a character trying to resolve very deep psychological difficulties—an addiction, a disability and its attendant social hardships, post traumatic stress disorder from Vietnam, or whatever shocks the human psyche is prone to.

You needn't include only one such dramatic mechanism, either. You can employ several at once or show the different aspects/problems in different books within the series.

The important thing to remember is that change should occur in the main character's situation with every book. Whether the change can be considered personal growth or not depends on the type of series. Sometimes, in sheer investigative novels, the main character doesn't have to grow, although he or she can't remain entirely stagnant. The variation might be a move to another city or a move to private practice from an agency. But some transition ought to appear in at least one element from one series book to another.

One of my favorite authors, Michael Mallory, who writes a short story series about Dr. Watson's second wife (*The Adventures of the Second Mrs. Watson*), reminds me that a lot can happen to the characters in what he calls "the white space " between the stories or novels. Many transformations can occur in that space, bringing up new situations or renewing old difficulties.

Fun for You, Too

If you're going to write a series, you ought to really enjoy your characters. If you don't, you will get bored with them and that boredom will show. One hears of writers who want to end a series while the publisher pushes for more of the same. Be sure to invent people who entertain you and try to find ways to keep the work fresh for yourself.

Changing the backgrounds to your books can help. Authors such as the delightful Sujata Massey, who writes about Rei Shimura, a California girl living in Japan, will choose unique themes or settings for each new series novel. Rei has been involved with such Japanese traditions as flower arranging, Zen meditation, manga comic books, and the antiques trade. That means a lot of research for Massey. But I don't think she minds her yearly trips to Japan at all. Not only do such shifts of focus keep the work new and engrossing for Massey, they do so for the reader as well.

Massey's Rei Shimura is a great character—lots of fun—but also to keep the series on the edge, Massey has given Rei two different boyfriends in the space of four books. Each relationship is real and endearing, but when Boyfriend One goes back to Scotland in the white space and Rei meets Boyfriend Two inside book three, the reader's attention begins to perk up.

Protagonists can also change jobs between books. In the first book of a series of mine, the hero, Eric Ryder, fresh from his stint as an Army Ranger, is an executive protection specialist. In book two, he's trying to upgrade his working conditions and markets himself as an information security specialist. Book three is from the point of view of his fiancé, Helen Robbins, an ex-Air Force pilot, who undertakes an investigation for the Private Plane Pilots Association. Writing a series book from the POV of a different protagonist isn't done much, so I advise great caution.

These developments were a lot of fun for me. I had covered industrial security for seven years as a trade journalist and had a lot of the information about executive protection and information security already, so I didn't need to do much research with the first two books.

Stay Flexible

Series can and will be sold, but they will also remain unsold and be canceled, so as much as you love writing a series, don't get overly attached. Your job description is "author." That means you are able to write about something else if this series doesn't work for a publisher. Even changing from one agent to another or one publisher to another can mean you must relinquish a beloved series. Rights can be the question in cases such as these. If your old agent will gain money from every book you sell in a particular series—even after you no longer deal with him or her—believe me you are going to want to ditch those characters. (So be careful what the contract says about your characters when you sign!)

Be ready to write not only your next in this series, as you are asked to, but to stop on a dime and go forward with a completely different sort of book. Writing the words is one part of your job. Using your imagination to come up with something new is another.

As my good friend Kit Sloane, author of *Final Cut* and *Grape Noir*, says: "Watch, listen, read, then write about it." Her first series, set among the horse set, was never picked up. Her series now going forward revolves around a Hollywood director/film editor couple.

7

On the Witness Stand

For the Record

I forced them to talk. I always force them to talk. I have my ways: I begged. They were kind and responded.

These are the experts, the writers who have been there—and are still there, publishing good books and reaping the rewards of this nearly impossible business. I whimpered piteously, until they shared their secrets with me, and with you.

Many I interviewed had similar comments to offer, although many disagreed with one another—and with me. That variance of opinions in itself makes a statement. Often, new writers are confused and want to know the "rules." But the rules are derived from our personal experiences and thoughts about what works. So if someone says to query 20 agents at once, and another top writer suggests sending a single inquiry at a time, you will have to decide for yourself what your approach will be. So, too, you will have to choose sides on many issues in the writing per se—considerations over which we authors express the greatest emotion. Bear in mind that you're the person ultimately responsible for what you do. You're your own authority.

As Socrates might once have said: "Pick your poison."

Elmore Leonard

Antiheroes His Specialty

The single, most salient fact about Elmore Leonard as a writer is that he is good—damn good. But even more wonderful for his fans—and those who dip into his novels and become his fans—is that unlike many other current authors who became stars years ago, Leonard has not at all burned out on writing.

Elmore Leonard still seems to take the greatest of pleasure in his work—and that joy of exercising his craft comes through in his novels.

Recently, Elmore Leonard obligingly consented to answer some questions I put to him. Here is the result.

G. Miki Hayden: What is your writing and publication schedule?

Elmore Leonard: I have two books out this year if you count the paperback edition of my previous hardcover, but I do only one a year. The paperback always follows a year later. It takes me four to five months to write one within a period of, say eight months with interruptions.

GMH: Why are most of your books set in Florida and California?

EL: I've used South Florida and Los Angeles as settings because I've spent a lot of time in both places. I have been going to Florida since 1950 and to L.A. since 1969. At first I went out to California to revise scripts, but more recently just for fun, to visit locations and watch my books filmed. I have quit doing screenplays, since I don't get that much satisfaction out of the process—or being an employee.

GMH: The books of yours that I've read are standalones. Why did you decide to write another Chili Palmer novel?

EL: MGM suggested a sequel to *Get Shorty* the night of the premier in Hollywood. Later on my publisher suggested the

music business as a setting and that appealed to me. The protagonist, Chili Palmer, was made to investigate what goes on in
that business. And the plot is actually a description of how I
work: assembling characters and seeing what kind of plot twists
and turns they might offer the story. I never begin with a complete idea; the ending remains a mystery to me until I get to it.

GMH: *Cuba Libre* is very different from your other books.
Why did you write it? It must have taken a lot of research.
EL: *Cuba Libre* isn't that much of a departure. I began my career
in the 50's writing westerns—eight novels and more than 30
short stories—so I had a good background for this one. A fasci-
nation with the Spanish American War led to the setting. It did
take a bit longer to write, about six months, mainly because of
the research involved. My researcher, Gregg Sutter, who lives in
Los Angeles, came up with everything I needed, and more. He's
been doing the heavy work since the early 80's.

GMH: Are you planning another novel of this type?
EL: I don't have a similar project in mind. I don't look any
farther ahead than the next book. A short story of mine called
"Sparks" in a Delacorte anthology, *Murder and Obsession*,
edited by Otto Penzler, got me thinking about my next book.
In the story is an insurance fraud investigator I thought could
be the protagonist of a novel. But now I'm thinking of it
more from the point of view of the antagonist, a woman
who comes out of prison with a desire to do stand-up comedy. At the moment I have no idea where the story might
go—or if it goes at all.

GMH: Anything else for your fans?

EL: I have a website that's loaded with information, even though I don't have a computer. I do all my writing in longhand.

Dale Furutani

Samurai of the Pen

Dale Furutani, like many mystery writers, is the epitome of graciousness and humor. I first met him online a number of years ago and then, later, in person at his signing for *The Toyotomi Blades* at the Black Orchid Bookstore in New York.

Since then, Dale has gone on to win much acclaim for his Ken Tanaka books—*Death in Little Tokyo* and *The Toyotomi Blades*. He received the 1997 Macavity Award given by Mystery Readers International (Best First Mystery Novel, *Death in Little Tokyo* from St. Martin's Press). He was nominated for an Agatha for 1997, won the 1997 Little Tokyo Author of the Year award, and was invited to speak at the U.S. Library of Congress, the Japanese American National Museum, The Wing Luke Asian Museum, and elsewhere. Despite his new and busy life, Dale has continued to be responsive and thoughtful to those who contact him.

In addition to his first series, Furutani has published a Samurai Mystery Trilogy, historical mysteries from William Morrow set in Japan in 1603, the year Tokugawa Ieyasu declared himself Shogun.

Here's what Dale has to say about it all:

G. Miki Hayden: How did you get started as a writer?
Dale Furutani: When I was in the fourth grade, we had 20 random words to learn for spelling drills. I was so bored by

this that I began writing little stories that used all the words. The teacher read these to the class, and I remember seeing the delighted looks on my classmates' faces as they listened. I was hooked on writing from then on. I'm still a lousy speller.

GMH: How does a writer learn to actually write?
DF: Taking classes and studying books are valuable, but they're not enough. Writing of any type—fiction, non-fiction, poetry, or notes on the Internet—all help you discover how to put one word after another into a cohesive narrative. And you have to write a lot. I think Ray Bradbury is the one who said the first million words don't count for much, and I believe that. On the other hand, books and classes are useful, a way of shortcutting the process instead of learning by pure trial and error. I have a degree in creative writing and I still buy and read books on the craft. I'm looking for the ideas, techniques, and the experiences of others to help me.

GMH: Can you give aspiring mystery writers some specific clues as to what to watch for regarding technique?
DF: I've noticed beginning mystery writers make several common mistakes. One is that they get so involved in the mechanics of plot that they forget the book should have some wonderful language. The details within a scene aren't enough. The scene should also be written in language that's fresh and entertaining. A second problem is that they trot out all that research they've done. Writers should communicate the minimum information necessary, not the maximum. Unless the detail is distinctive or telling, it shouldn't be there. A third error is not striving for a distinctive voice. It's easier to write faux Raymond Chandler or Agatha Christie than

develop your own written voice, but very few people can produce good Raymond Chandler or Agatha Christie. Authors are better off seeking their own style in their work.

GMH: How about getting an agent?

DF: You have to approach the agent search professionally, instead of just firing off blind letters to listings. I researched my agent as carefully as I research a book. I found several writers I admire—not all mystery writers by the way—and then tried to discover who their agents were. That wasn't always easy, but if you can track down the editor at their publisher, you can usually get the agent's name. I found one agent who represented two authors I like and contacted her. A few weeks later, she was my agent. I never had to go down the rest of the list I had put together, but I was prepared if my first choice didn't agree to represent me. By the way, at conferences I make a point of talking to agents or asking other authors how they like their agent. I'm perfectly happy with mine, but if I ever have to change agents, I'll be ready. That's part of being professional in your approach to the business of writing.

GMH: What's the most important thing a mystery writer should do to promote? How did you use special contacts, for instance?

DF: The sad fact is that very few writers are going to get extensive support from a publisher and it's now part of the profession for authors to engage in self-promotion. You can rely on the strength of your writing to get you noticed, but with so many new books every year, this simply may not happen. You have to get people reading your work before they can decide if they like it.

Because I've been successful at promotion, some people think I had special contacts when I started. I didn't. I did have an MBA in marketing to go along with my undergraduate degree in creative writing, so I was realistic about the need to promote. From the very beginning, I felt my work could have appeal outside the mystery community and I actively pursued these areas. As a result, the Japanese-American, Asian, and literary communities have lent support to my work that mysteries don't normally get. I think every author or book has similar ties outside of mysteries, if they're thought about and pursued. How do you try to find contacts outside of mysteries? The same way you look for them within the mystery community. You contact people, tell them about yourself and your work, and seek opportunities to do signings, panels, or talks. A significant percentage of people who buy my books aren't really mystery buffs, so pursuing these communities has been worthwhile.

GMH: Did it take you a long time to get published?
DF: That depends on how you want to look at it. Like a lot of people, I had poetry and short pieces published when I was in school. In high school, I started writing non-fiction articles for money, and that's how I worked my way through college. I was a creative writing major, but I didn't have the slightest idea how to make a living at fiction when I graduated. Despite some early encouragement, I had no sales, so I stopped writing fiction for over 20 years and continued to write nonfiction.

When I started writing mystery novels, publication actually came very fast. Finding an agent and getting offers for

Death in Little Tokyo took only a few weeks. I guess you can either say it took me 20 years or it took me only a matter of weeks for my first fiction sale.

GMH: Since your Ken Tanaka series is contemporary mystery, what made you decide to do an historical series?

DF: I've always had an interest in history, and I thought combining that interest with my mystery writing would be fun. I selected a trilogy because I wanted to examine particular aspects of ancient Japan. The first book of three is set in a remote mountain village, the second book is set on the great Tokaido Road, and third book is set in Edo, the capital of the newly proclaimed Shogun, Tokugawa Ieyasu.

GMH: How did you do your research?

DF: Well, I added approximately 100 books to my library to help with the research, including some pretty obscure scholarly studies dealing with Japanese village social structure, how they built Japanese farmhouses, or the court system in the Tokugawa era. Despite the large number of tomes, sticking my nose in a book isn't the primary way I research the series.

I've been to Japan fifteen or sixteen times (I've lost count of the exact number). After I saw all the standard tourist stuff, I started tracking down more obscure locations. When I got the idea for this trilogy, I started visiting folk museums and the old sections of towns like Kamakura. I wanted to walk the streets I was writing about, learn about the details of life, and, as much as possible, experience what my characters experience. This has sometimes gotten me some weird stares as I've done things like track down the location of the old brothel district in Tokyo (Edo). This was actually harder than it might sound, because the famous brothel district of Edo, Yoshiwara, was founded 50 years after the time of my story! By the way, in case you're wondering, the old brothel district is now famous as a location where they make children's dolls.

I've also talked to scholars, people at the Library of Congress and, on my next trip to Japan, I hope to meet with a descendant of Tokugawa Ieyasu, who has promised to show me some family treasures. I don't intend my trilogy to be a work of scholarship, because there are many fine non-fiction books that cover Japanese history, but, as much as possible, I do want things to be accurate.

GMH: Anything else you'd like to say?
DF: Yes. Many things. You'll find them in my upcoming books.

Sujata Massey

Looking to the Past for Her Clues

Her first novel, published in 1997, was *The Salaryman's Wife*, which won an Agatha and was nominated for an Anthony. The novel received a lot of other positive attention as well, such as being chosen as a Page Turner of the Week by *People Magazine*, a not inconsiderable salute. Others in her wonderfully charming series have been *Zen Attitude*, *The Flower Master*, and *The Floating Girl*.

Salaryman's protagonist, Rei Shimura, is a California girl of Japanese ancestry, who now lives in Tokyo where she first taught English and has gone on to selling antiques. There are no stock characters in Massey's work, but each personality is completely detailed, believable, and quirky! Her plots are intricately woven, and unwind at a leisurely, but perfectly paced tempo. For those interested in Japan—and most readers will be by the end of her books—Massey gives the absolutely contemporary version, complete with today's complex mix of the traditional, spiced by the American military/business flavoring that landed in Japan more than half a century ago.

I had a chat with the beautiful Sujata Massey upon her return to the East Coast from the scorching wilds of Texas, where she literally fought off scorpions in order to sign for her fans at ClueFest held there in July.

G. Miki Hayden: Considering that your background is other than the one you depict, why did you choose a Japanese/California woman as a protagonist?

Sujata Massey: I was born in England to parents from India and Germany, and when I was five our family emigrated to the U.S. I have never known what it was like to belong firmly to one ethnic group, so when it came time to choose a narrator for my first mystery, I decided to make her bicultural, Western and Asian, so I could address some issues of what it means to belong to more than one country. I made half of Rei's heritage Japanese because I'd lived there for two years, spending most of my time in the Tokyo suburbs getting to know housewives and people connected with traditional arts. My Japanese women friends taught me a lot about family life and expectations for women, which I used to form Rei's social background.

GMH: When did you first conceive these books?

SM: I moved to Japan in 1991 as the new bride of a young Navy medical officer. While my husband was at sea for 14

out of our 24-month tour, I decided to do something significant. I had thought of writing nonfiction articles for a memoir
about my times in Japan, but I quickly realized that the literary market was glutted with such things. I had written fiction in college and decided to give it a try once more.

GMH: Why mysteries? Are you a long-time mystery
reader?
SM: I have read mysteries since childhood, starting with
some English children's series by the late writer Enid Blyton
and graduated to Sir Arthur Conan Doyle and Agatha
Christie by the time I was in junior high. I was again drawn
to mystery when, as an undergraduate writing major at
Johns Hopkins University, I took a small workshop taught
by the author Martha Grimes. It wasn't until I reached Japan
that I began reading mysteries set in the United States as
well as the United Kingdom! I think that my early indoc-
trination into English mysteries has stamped my work in a
peculiar way.

GMH: When did you first start writing fiction?
SM: I had written some novels that could loosely be classified as "romantic suspense" in junior high. My sisters started
snooping in my manuscripts and began quoting the most
purple, embarrassing lines in front of other people, so I
stopped writing. I studied short story writing in college during the "minimalist" era. We were schooled in writing little
stories about very small issues—to make the writing the
focus of the story rather than the plot. This style of fiction
didn't come naturally to me, and while I took my B-plus or
whatever the famous novelist professor doled out, I told

myself that someday I would write a novel to please myself. At the ripe old age of 27, when I was newly married and unemployed in Japan, it was the time to try fiction once more. I spent four years writing *The Salaryman's Wife*.

GMH: How many times do you draft a book?

SM: Because I was learning to write mystery while working on *The Salaryman's Wife*, I did probably 50 full drafts of the book. I kept polishing until I was fairly happy with it. My rewriting obsession is no doubt a product of my five years in journalism, where one kept altering the story until the editor found it acceptable for publication. I always believed that you could turn a molehill into a mountain! *Zen Attitude* came much easier for me; I think I only did four drafts. *The Flower Master*, out in 1999, was also a four-draft book. Four is an unlucky number in Japan, but maybe it's my lucky number for writing.

GMH: What would you like to tell people who want to write a mystery?

SM: Until recently, some editors and other publishing people proclaimed that mysteries with foreign settings don't sell. They thought that readers could not understand foreign names or have the patience to learn about their cultures. When *The Salaryman's Wife* was published, I found out that people were passionately interested in Japan, and my readers often had a friend or family member who had studied or worked there, so it felt fairly familiar for them to read about walking on *tatami* mats or eating sushi from a conveyor belt. Readers have a hunger for books set in unusual places; I've been asked by some readers to take Rei elsewhere in Asia, and even to Europe! What this says to me is that writers who have a genuine connection to other countries and cultures should not be afraid to explore that in their fiction.

GMH: How does a new writer go about getting an agent?

SM: I decided to pursue agents who had a marked pattern of representing good mystery writers. I gathered names from the acknowledgments of some of my favorite mystery novels, then gathered more by checking the attendee list of various conferences, such as Malice Domestic. Finally, I asked the few editors and writers I knew if those agents had a good reputation. The one thing I didn't do was go to a published friend and say, "Can I send my book to your agent?" I think that tactic is likely to make the writer feel used. It's better to ask the writer's opinion of an agent who is not her own. Then, if she feels like it, she might spontaneously offer contact with her own agent.

I believe an author's enthusiasm about another writer means very little to the agents. Over the years, I've recommended at least six unpublished writers to my own agent, who read their manuscripts but only wound up taking on one of them. This particular book was never sold. Since I wasn't very effective in helping the unpublished authors ultimately sell their work, I recommend that writers do their own research in finding an agent.

GMH: What's the most important thing a mystery writer should do to promote?

SM: The two areas that writers should think about are signing books, and having their book reviewed in the media.

Either your publisher assigns a publicity person to set up signings for you, or you set them up yourself. I usually do a combination—agree to do the few signings my publicist arranges, then put on my thinking cap and come up with a lot of other possibilities, some out of town, and call the bookstores myself to see if they'd like me to visit. I find that signing in tandem with another author usually makes for a better turnout.

As for media attention—if you can get your publisher to give you a lot of ARCs (bound advance reading copies of the book) a few months before the book comes out, you can send them to reviewers/press people you think might be interested. Include a targeted cover letter about yourself and photocopies of any other media features or reviews of your work. I spent hours writing personalized letters and sending out ARCs to various press people when I wrote my first two mysteries, and these are the books that wound up being reviewed in *People* and *USA Today*. You are your own best publicist. The trick is not to come off as a pushy self-promoter in your materials; be polite, businesslike, and let your book speak for itself.

William Kent Krueger

Newcomer Thrills With Action/Real Characters

William Kent Krueger was a success from the start, breaking into hardcover with his very first release, an honor generally reserved for better-established authors. Independent mystery bookdealers nominated each of his titles as a book that year which was most fun to sell. Perhaps even more gratifying, mystery fans awarded him an Anthony in 1999 in the category of Best First, for his series start, *Iron Lake*. Once a logger and construction worker, then a college administrator, Krueger now writes full-time. His second novel out is *Boundary Waters*.

G. Miki Hayden: The geographic background is integral to your novels. How did you choose it?

William Kent Krueger: My family moved around a lot when I was a kid. When I first set foot in Minnesota, at the age of thirty, I felt as if I'd finally found home. Moving to Minnesota so that my wife could attend law school also seemed to spur my writing and I began to set the stories I was working on here, and in the rest of the Midwest. When I finally decided it was time to try my hand at a novel, Minnesota was a natural choice. I knew that whatever manuscript I ultimately created, it would be in part a homage to this place that has become my adopted homeland.

GMH: Did you do much research on the Native Americans you wrote about?

WKK: I briefly attended Stanford University and, while there, became interested in anthropology. As a result, when I decided to set my first novel in northern Minnesota—and realized that I couldn't really do that without including the Anishinaabe people as a major element—I was excited by the prospect of researching their lives. I read everything I could about the Ojibwe in Minnesota, and when I sat down to pen the novel, tried very hard to be sensitive to the fact that, despite my research, I would always be writing from outside the culture. After I'd completed the manuscript, I asked two Ojibwe readers to look it over and comment. They were very helpful, and also very complimentary.

GMH: How did you pick the protagonist?
WKK: I knew I wanted a protagonist who was struggling in many ways. Adding a crisis in his own cultural identity to the other problems in his life, would deepen, I believed, his complexity as a character, and also provide infinite material to explore as the series progressed. I toyed with combinations—Ojibwe/Italian, Ojibwe/Scandinavian—until I met a woman who was part Ojibwe Anishinaabe and part Irish. I liked that particular combination. And Corcoran Liam O'Connor was born.

GMH: When did you start writing, and why?
WKK: I've always written. My parents were very encouraging. In my twenties, I made writing a part of my discipline every day, and it has served me well. As for the why, I cannot really say. Mostly, I feel as I've had no choice in the matter. It's always been something I do that makes me happy.

GMH: How easy or hard was it for you to get published?
WKK: I was extremely fortunate in this regard. When my agent, Jane Jordan Browne, submitted the manuscript for *Iron Lake* to the New York publishing houses, a bidding war erupted between Pocket Books and St. Martin's. It was an author's dream come true.

GMH: I know you write short stories, but can you tell me a little about how you came to write short mystery and your progression there?

WKK: I've always believed short stories were a wonderful training ground for writers. A short story can be almost wholly comprised of a single portion of a writer's arsenal—mostly dialog, for example, or character study—so it offers a great opportunity to focus on honing particular skills. It's also a very refreshing venue, because a short story may be created in as little as a single sitting (though rarely for me). I do mystery short stories mostly on demand now, at the request of an editor who is putting together an anthology, and I look forward to it as a kind of test. Can I come up with a suitable story to meet the particular requirements of the anthology? Although I much prefer the freedom offered by the larger scope of a novel, I always appreciate the opportunity and challenge of writing a short story.

GMH: Did recognition of your first novel change your life?
WKK: I've had only two life changing experiences. Marriage and the birth of my children. Both have been wonderful. The recognition that *Iron Lake* has brought has been extremely gratifying. However, when I sit down with my notebook every morning to work on whatever my current project happens to be, I'm faced with the same uncertainty, the same fear of failure that has always plagued me. The best result of publication of *Iron Lake* and *Boundary Waters* has been my introduction to the mystery community that includes other authors, booksellers, and readers. It's a wonderful community to be a part of.

GMH: What's coming out next?
WKK: The third Cork O' Connor mystery, titled *Purgatory Ridge*, was released in January 2001.

GMH: What are you working on now?

WKK: I'm halfway through my fourth manuscript, which is a standalone. Although I'm using many of the elements that readers seem to enjoy in my other books, i.e., the Minnesota landscape, I'm trying some new things, attempting to grow as a writer. I'll return to the Cork O'Connor series as soon as this manuscript is completed.

Laura Lippman

Siren of Baltimore: Edgar Winner and Journalist

First she belted out *Baltimore Blues* (Avon, February 1997), then mesmerized us with the second in her Tess Monoghan series, *Charm City*—the name Baltimore boosters use for their town. Third came the equally seductive *Butcher's Hill*, entitled after an actual Baltimore section (and not a reference to a murder). After *In Big Trouble*, which sent Tess to San Antonio, Lippman's protagonist headed back to her hometown in *The Sugar House*, the first hardcover for Tess, issued by Morrow. Next up is *Strange City*, slated for fall 2001, with another to come in fall 2002.

Lippman's list of honors for these titles is a long one, amounting to 13 nominations for prestigious mystery awards. Every book of the series has received some of these kudos. *Charm City* won the Edgar and the Shamus, while *Butcher's Hill* won the Anthony and the Agatha.

"This roll call strikes me as unseemly," blushes Lippman, "but I am pleased that I've been honored both by my peers, who read for the Edgar and the Shamus, and the fans, who choose the Anthony and the Agatha winners. Clearly, I wouldn't have so many nominations if it weren't for contests that recognize the paperback original, but the Agatha and the Macavity don't have such categories and it means a lot to me that I became one of the few paperback writers to win Best Novel at Malice Domestic."

Laura Lippman continues to work as a freelance writer at the *Baltimore Sun*, interviewing the literary likes of Doris Lessing, James Ellroy, Erica Jong, and Walter Mosley. Her work is often syndicated nationally, and in 1996 the local city magazine named her as *The Sun's* best writer. Laura and I, who have known each other for a number of years, spoke recently.

G. Miki Hayden: Your premier work of mystery fiction was *Baltimore Blues*. Was this, in fact, the first you had written?

Laura Lippman: In my twenties, I tried my hand at the kind of sensitive, autobiographical novels that so many young women in their twenties attempt. Luckily I never inflicted those on the world. I knew I needed a story to tell, a reason for the reader to go from page 1 to page 300. I found that story in my fleeting fantasy of killing a friend's boss. Then I nursed the idea for this novel for years, like a secret grudge, until my husband's confidence in me—and a new computer—inspired me to finally write the book that became *Baltimore Blues*.

GMH: There's often a long process between writing that novel and having it published. How did that work for you?

LL: When I finished my book, I showed it to a friend, Michele Slung, an editor who knows everything about mysteries and just about everybody in mystery publishing. She helped me find my agent, Vicky Bijur. On Vicky's recommendation, I made a few minor revisions and she then submitted it to 10 publishers, three of which bid. I signed a two-book contract.

GMH: You write about books for *The Sun*, and are considered to have rather highbrow tastes. Why do you choose to write mysteries?

LL: My friends who have yet to see the light—in other words, don't realize the incredible depth and breadth of mysteries—often ask me the same thing. Well, I wrote a mystery because I had an idea for a mystery. In the way that it so often happens, the story chose the teller. I got lucky in journalism and didn't lose my job at a crucial time, as so many of my friends did. But I started thinking about Robert Frost's two roads in the yellow wood and imagined the life of a young woman who had ended up on the path I wasn't forced to explore. If she couldn't be a reporter, then maybe she could be a private detective, which is what Tess decided to do. It should be noted that I started writing my first book when I was miserable over layoffs at the paper. *Baltimore Blues* comes by its depressed quality quite honestly.

GMH: *Charm City* is about the newspaper business. Did something specific inspire the story?

LL: *Charm City* is a pretty personal book. I had a retired racing greyhound, whom I came to love dearly. She became an important character and plot line in this book. And after going through a tough merger of *The Sun* and *The Evening Sun*, I had a lot of feelings bottled up inside me about newspapers. As an *Evening Sun* reporter, I was persona non grata. After a bruising period in which I was told repeatedly I was just no good, I wrote a piece for the 60th anniversary of

James Cain's *The Postman Always Rings Twice*. That story proved to be my "audition" for the features department. I moved to features four months later, where I was given a chance to reinvent my career. My professional fortunes have been wonderful ever since. But I've seen other friends driven out of the business.

GMH: Do you think of Tess as your alter ego, or is she acting out a certain side of you that is usually unexpressed?

LL: Tess and I have a complicated relationship. She's not me, and yet she's also not not me. Have you ever met a younger person who reminds you of yourself, someone who inspires equal parts exasperation and nostalgia? That's how I feel about Tess. I see her making all the mistakes I made and I want to shout out to her, but she can't hear me and even if she could, she'd pay no heed. She just knows she's right.

GMH: What are your work habits? Do you get up at 3 am and write? Write every day, or only when you have the time? Need constant trips to the kitchen while you work? Watch television in between sentences (me)?

LL: I get up at 6, eat breakfast and then head into my study. I listen to music while I write—not that I really hear it—and work steadily for two hours. At 8:30, I shower and go to work. On weekends, I get to sleep later, but the routine is pretty much the same. Sometimes, especially when the end is in sight, I'll take a week's "vacation" and do nothing but write. That feels incredibly luxurious.

GMH: What is the hardest part of plotting a mystery? Do you know the end before you begin?

LL: I start out knowing who the killer is and why he or she killed. I sometimes write pretty extensive outlines, although I didn't at one time. The trick is trying to get Tess to figure out what I know myself. I have this image of a person crossing a stream, jumping from rock to rock. I think the hardest thing is layering a book with surprises, but still playing fair.

GMH: What is not playing fair in a mystery?

LL: Oh, incredible twists, impossible plot points. But, as a reader, if a book is so good that I don't second-guess it until about 90 seconds after I've finished the last page, I think the writer has pulled it off. It's when I start saying, "Hey wait a minute!" while I'm reading that I get annoyed. Like many Chandler fans, I'm familiar with the story about how no one could figure out the plot of *The Big Sleep*—including Chandler. But that doesn't bother me. It's the stories that ask me to suspend belief every page of the way, or the ones where you can see the gears, that annoy me.

GMH: Any other theories of mystery writing?

LL: I'm not sure I have theories, per se, but I have some very strong convictions. I never want to write a "menace" scene in a parking garage. I don't want to write stories in which child molestation drives the plot. As for serial killers—well, Thomas Harris set the bar pretty high with *Red Dragon*. I've used a serial killer as a secondary character, but he was actually pretty pathetic, not a criminal mastermind.

I do have one theory: The best mysteries have at least one scene that resonates, that remains in your head after the rest of the plot has faded—a little freeze frame that you can't forget.

GMH: How does a writer learn to actually write?

LL: By reading. So read well, because the books you choose are going to teach you how to write. And by practicing, by which I guess I mean drafting and redrafting. If you accept the fact that you can't get it right the first time, you free yourself to make the kind of mistakes and errors that lead to a greater understanding of the story you're trying to tell.

GMH: Can you give aspiring mystery writers some specific clues as to what to watch for regarding technique?

LL: Use all your senses. I've noticed that some beginning writers create visually stunning worlds, but the other senses are strangely absent. It's like watching a silent film. Also, don't assume that great writing or wonderful characters can cover up sloppy plotting. Yes, there are dozens of examples of books where the writers are so dazzling that we forgive the holes in their plots, but I don't think anyone aims to write a less-than-credible story.

GMH: How about getting an agent?

LL: I do believe writers should have agents, and I think it's really easy to do. Read the acknowledgments in books and, if necessary, the Hot Deals column in Publishers Weekly to find the names of agents. Write a one-page query letter. Sit back and wait. If you've done your homework right, some of the agents you've queried will want to read your manuscript. Don't pay a reading fee to anyone.

GMH: What's the most important thing a mystery writer should do to promote?

LL: Promotion matters, yet I've never been able to figure out what really helps, so I can only recommend what I've done.

Go to conventions. Get to the independent mystery bookstores. Line up speaking gigs. Think small—yes, it would be nice to be on the cover of the *New York Times Book Review*, but that's probably not within your control. However, you can send your book to small regional daily and weekly newspapers, and those little mentions have a cumulative effect. The most important thing is to be nice. Truly.

GMH: As Barbara Walters asks her subjects, what would you most like people to say about you?

LL: I find myself torn. My instinct is to say something namby-pamby, like "Oh, I hope they think I'm nice." Instead, I believe I'd prefer: "How does someone who seems so nice write such wicked books?" Failing that, I'll settle for: "I had no idea Baltimore was such an interesting place."

S.J. Rozan

Author With a Hard Hat

S. J. Rozan is the author of the Lydia Chin/Bill Smith books, which include her most recent work, *Reflecting the Sky*, and the other six in the series: *Stone Quarry*, *A Bitter Feast*, *No Colder Place* (winner of the Anthony and nominated for the Shamus award for Best Novel), *Mandarin Plaid*, *Concourse* (which won a Shamus award for Best Novel) and *China Trade*. The protagonists also appear in a number of short stories, including "Hoops," a 1997 Edgar nominee.

Born and brought up in the Bronx, Rozan is an architect

in a NewYork firm where she gets to work on police stations, firehouses, zoo buildings, and the largest terra cotta restoration project in the world. A Knicks fan and a self-confessed point guard, Rozan has worked as a martial arts instructor, jewelry saleswoman, and janitor.

G. Miki Hayden: How does a writer learn to actually write?
S.J. Rozan: By reading. And by writing. And by deliberately trying things—changes in rhythm, odd uses of words—and seeing how they work. If you play basketball every day, you're a basketball player and you'll learn and improve. If you watch basketball every day, you're not and you won't.

GMH: Can you give aspiring mystery writers some specific clues as to what to watch for regarding technique?
SJR: Avoid the verb "to be," especially in the formation "there was," such as "There was a glove on the floor." This sentence format invariably comes off as weak. Avoid adverbs. Nouns and verbs matter most; adjectives matter somewhat but should not be used to bolster sagging nouns or verbs. People almost always say things; they almost never remark, retort, or quip.

GMH: How about getting an agent?
SJR: Find out who the agent was for books similar to yours that you enjoyed. Call the publisher's rights department and ask; they'll tell you. Write a one-page combination intro and query letter—this is who I am, this is what my book is. Don't be puppy-like ("Please, please read my book.") or arrogant ("Do yourself a favor and read my book because it'll make both of us lots of money."). Be a pro.

GMH: What's the most important thing a mystery writer should do to promote? How did you use special contacts, for instance?

SJR: Be nice to everybody. When someone asks you to do a gig, say yes. If the gig doesn't work out well, stay good-natured, at least in public. If only three people turn up for a reading, read for them—they're the ones who came. Don't try to get people to do you favors—do them favors. When the Chinatown History Museum gave me a reading, I made sure at least 20 people in the audience were friends of mine who were not on the CHM mailing list. The CHM felt that it had made new contacts that way.

Linda Fairstein

So Real You Can Smell the Blood

Any commentary on Linda Fairstein's writing has to start off (and end) with a discussion of the author herself. That's because Fairstein is the spitting image of her protagonist, Assistant District Attorney Alexandra Cooper, head of New York City's Sex Crimes Prosecution Unit. Yes, Alex Cooper's creator has herself been chief of that very unit since 1976 and has, from that post, successfully prosecuted some of the biggest cases in the nation, such as the Preppie Murder and Central Park Jogger cases.

In her novels, Fairstein delights the detail-hungry reader with a true insider's view of the criminal justice system in a city that sees many of the most sensational and horrifying crimes in the world. We've read these types of descriptions in the fiction of Ed McBain and others, and have seen it on the tube in *NYPD Blue*, but we'll never get quite so close as Fairstein takes us, and that, in itself, is of maximum interest.

Fairstein takes the time in her fiction to educate us in the realities of sex crimes and their prosecution—and the progress that has been made in the past 20 or so years. Fairstein's first book in 1993, *Sexual Violence: Our War Against Rape*, was a nonfiction account of her prosecutorial work, a book that made an impressive splash and was a *New York Times* Notable. This feat was followed in 1996 by the first Alex Cooper mystery-thriller, *Final Jeopardy*, after which came *Likely to Die* and then *Cold Hit*.

An interview with the very down-to-earth, crime-busting Fairstein garnered some (undisclosable but fascinating) tidbits regarding high-profile city crimes, as well as the true scoop on this public figure's fabulous dual career.

G. Miki Hayden: Why fiction?

Linda Fairstein: I always dreamed of writing fiction. I've written all my life—majored in English Literature in college and truly love the process of creating a work and playing with the language. I've always been a voracious reader, and enjoy anything that keeps me in and around books. Originally, several publishers asked me to write about my work, which became the nonfiction book I published with Morrow in 1993. The funny thing is that each publisher assumed the book would have to be written by a ghostwriter. Then, by the time I sat down and wrote it myself, I was spurred on to what I had always dreamed of—to write in the genre I most enjoy: crime novels and murder mysteries.

GMH: Why did you choose to be a prosecutor? Why sex crimes?

LF: By the time I graduated from Vassar and entered law school at the University of Virginia, I knew that I wanted to perform public service for a while. I became fascinated with criminal law and the justice system. The best training ground in the country for trial lawyers was always the Manhattan D.A.'s office, so I applied. At the time, there were almost two hundred lawyers here, only seven of whom were woman. The D.A. told me the job was "too tawdry" for me. I've obviously thrived on tawdriness. The work has been enormously rewarding, and endlessly challenging.

At the time I started here, there was no such thing as a sex crime unit anywhere in the country. In 1974, this one opened with two assistant D.A.'s. When I was asked to take over the unit two years later, my initial response was to say "no," thinking that a steady diet of one kind of crime would be boring. My boss pressed on, promising me that if I got the unit running for a year or so, he'd give me another assignment. Needless to say, I fell in love with the work and it's what has kept me here all these years.

GMH: Where do Alex Cooper and Linda Fairstein overlap?

LF: I'm frequently asked how much of me is mixed with Alex Cooper. I've taken great liberties with her personal side—ah, fiction!—making her younger, thinner and blonder, and endowing her with a trust fund to give her the freedom to move around in ways that young prosecutors really can't do on our salaries. The question of identities has even been confusing to some of my good friends. Since Coop's voice is so much like my own, they frequently ask, "Is that true, were you really engaged to that medical student when we were in law school?" On the other hand, Coop's professional views are drawn very much from my own, and she reflects my passion about this job. I felt that one thing I could contribute to this genre was the authenticity of the unique work I've been involved with for a quarter of a century.

GMH: Do you take material from your real-life cases?
LF: In each of the three books I've completed, the murder around which the story centers is something I have created myself. But I do take a lot of material from my real life experience, and from cases that cross my desk every day.

GMH: What's next?
LF: I'm still promoting the third book in the series, Cold Hit, which involves the murder of a New York art dealer. This takes Coop, Chapman, and Wallace into the world of galleries, museum heists, and auction bid rigging. The art world seems like such an elegant milieu on the surface, but it's teeming with unsavory characters, frauds, and stolen paintings.

The term "cold hit," by the way, is a new forensic expression. It's what scientists refer to when a computer matches a DNA sample to a human being even before the police consider that person a suspect. Here, I use it as a double enendre—since the murder may be a "hit," too.

GMH: So do you have some non-series ideas?
LF: I hope the series goes on and on, of course, but I also have non-series ideas, such as a book with Mike Chapman as the main character, so I'd love to do one from his point of view.

Also, I'd love to do something different—more of a courtroom/legal thriller than my series, which I consider to be procedurals. There is one old case of mine in particular that I would like to explore in that way . . . down the road a piece.

GMH: How does a writer learn to actually write?
LF: Most people who become writers do so, in part, because they have always derived pleasure from the use of the language. If you don't like reading, if you aren't fascinated by the range of magnificent images created by words, then I don't think you will ever enjoy the process of writing. With time, we all refine our tastes and gravitate towards styles or genres we like to read, but a good writer has an almost omnivorous taste for brilliant examples of the language. Then, sooner or later, you must simply put pen to paper and write. I'm always amazed by the number of people I encounter who tell me they want to write books, but actually hate to write. You have to like the actual experience of writing. It is difficult, it is lonely, it is unforgiving—but if you enjoy doing it, it is an extraordinarily self-fulfilling art. So write. Every day.

GMH: Can you give aspiring mystery writings some specific clues as to what to watch for regarding technique?
LF: I think aspiring mystery writers need to sample the genre and find the style of book that appeals to them. Most of us who write crime novels do so because we have read them for pleasure. I think it's important to find a voice that is closest to what the writer hopes to accomplish in telling her or his story, and try to get comfortable telling tales in that voice.

GMH: How about getting an agent?

LF: For an unpublished writer, this is perhaps the single most difficult step. Most of the great agents do not accept over-the-transom work. Use any contact you have to get your work under the nose of a good agent or editor, and that includes going through some of the more generous, established writers, who often enjoy reaching a hand out to someone just getting started.

GMH: What's the most important thing a mystery writer should do to promote?

LF: One has to be willing, I think, to go almost anywhere and do almost anything—professional, not crazy—to help promote the book. One thing that helps a lot is that the mystery community, with its core of small, independent bookstores, fans, and newsletters, is a very solid and friendly one. Word of mouth is important, and being willing to build slowly is critical, too. There are very few overnight success stories and you need to accept the fact that a slow, steady growth is the likely path—and a lucky one to have, at that.

Larry Karp

Music to the Mystery Reader's Ears

Larry Karp, M.D., began his writing career with the thriller *Genetic Engineering: Threat or Promise?*, a book for the non-medical reading public. Perhaps the work wasn't much of a mystery—but then neither was *The View from the Vue*, about Karp's experiences at Bellevue Hospital as a med student, intern, and resident back in the 60s. His *The Enchanted Ear*, real-life stories about music box enthusiasts, however, was a sort of precursor to his current series, since Karp's protagonist Thomas Purdue is rabid about these particular antiques.

After about eight to ten rejections of Karp's first mystery novel, an author-friend suggested the independent publisher Write Way, which snapped up the book. This work, The Music Box Murders, was a finalist for the Romance Writers of America's Daphne Du Maurier award. The next in the series, Scamming the Birdman, sets a slightly different pace by being a caper story, rather than a mystery. The Midnight Special, the third Purdue adventure, was issued in March 2001 to strongly positive reviews. The fourth Purdue novel, The Sorcerer and the Junkman, is scheduled for April 2002.

G. Miki Hayden: How does a writer learn to actually write?

Larry Karp: Read critically. Ask questions; give yourself specific answers. Exactly why do you like some books and dislike others? What did an author do that made a plot work? What techniques caused a book to fall flat? What made a fictional person come alive on the page? What made a character come across as a cardboard chess-piece, its author's hand clearly visible with every move? Read dialog aloud. Can you tell which fictional person is speaking? Do stilted lines make it impossible for you to believe in the speaker as a flesh-and-blood individual? A year or so of writing classes with a competent instructor may help, but after that, ask yourself whether you're using the classes as a social activity, or even as therapy. At that point, maybe it's better to work individually with a writing professional, getting help as needed with particular problems.

Just write. Don't talk about your writing. Not to anyone, except to your designated consultant. There's no better way of letting all the energy out of your work than telling people what you're doing and how you're going about it. Besides, most of your listeners really don't care.

GMH: Why did you decide to write a mystery series?

LK: I started out to write a mainstream novel set among the music box collecting crowd, but the protagonist insisted on getting knocked off on page one. So I decided I must be writing a mystery novel, and proceeded accordingly. Some three years later, I finished *Music Box Murders*, and felt really, really depressed without my characters around anymore. Write a series? I wondered. Nah. I didn't want to do the same thing over and over. Then I visited in my head with my protagonist one hot June afternoon, and in runs this guy with a big red bristly mustache, hollering something about his collection's been stolen and he's going to kill Vincent LoPriore, that son of a bitch! What do you think, I have dumb characters? They wanted to keep living as much as I wanted them to.

GMH: Can you give aspiring mystery writers some specific clues as to what to watch for regarding technique?

LK: Story comes first. Endless authorial ranting or maundering by a fictional person about some particular evil in our society indicates that you're probably writing a tract, not a story. You want to outrage your audience? Just show a lovely, innocent person badly hurt or killed because of the societal fault you detest—but don't remark on it. That'll get 'em every time. Pay attention to your story. Where is it trying to take you? Don't force your prejudices and biases onto the story. Let go, go along, listen. One of the greatest joys in writing is to look at a line that just popped up on the screen (or onto the page, however you may write) and say, "Where did that come from? Is that what I think?"

Listen to your fictional people. Live in their world, even when you're not actually writing. Just as you don't know everything about anyone in your real world, you don't know everything about your fictional friends (and enemies) either. The more time you spend with them and the better you get to know them, the more they'll surprise and amaze you. Every now and then a fictional person will get a bit cheeky, try to take the story over, but you can handle that. Make a deal with him or her: Do your job or die. Either way, the author wins.

GMH: How about getting an agent?

LK: Getting an agent is very nice, but it's also very difficult. Agents want you to be published; publishers want you to be agented. In addition, getting an agent does not guarantee success. I know many unpublished writers who've gone through several agents. Try to get an agent, sure, but meanwhile, send your work out on your own. Try the independent (formerly called "small") press. You won't get rich, but life with the independents has many advantages. By the way, I still don't have an agent but have three mystery novels in print, with a fourth due out. I'm satisfied.

GMH: What's the most important thing a mystery writer should do to promote?

LK: First, buy a copy of Kate Derie's *Deadly Directory* (Deadly Serious Press, Tucson, Arizona or Cluelass.com). Booksellers, events, publications, publishers, organizations—they're all there. That'll be the best tax-deductible money you'll ever spend. Then work like hell. Go for the personal touch. There're a lot of mystery books out there, but there are also a lot of mystery readers, and if you can interest them in your work, they'll read it. If they like it, they'll tell other people. Schedule appearances at your local bookstores and libraries. Don't take a trip without setting up readings or signings. Mystery bookshops love having authors come by. Surprisingly, many of the chain stores are receptive as well. Go to conferences such as Left Coast Crime, Malice Domestic, Bouchercon, and many others. Volunteer for panel appearances and readings. Aside from promoting your work, you'll meet a whole new bunch of people, mostly very nice, and have a good time in the bargain. Oh, and yes. Then go home and write.

Rick Riordan

Teacher From Texas Who Kills With Great Flair

Rick Riordan is the author of the Tres Navarre mystery series. His first novel *Big Red Tequila* won the Anthony award for Best Paperback Original and the Shamus award for Best First Private Eye Novel. His second novel, *The Widower's Two-Step*, won the Edgar award for Best Paperback Original. His most recent Tres Navarre mystery is *The Devil Went Down to Austin* (Bantam hardcover, June 2001). Riordan's short fiction has appeared in *Mary Higgins Clark Mystery Magazine* and *The Shamus Game*. In addition to writing, Riordan teaches middle school English in San Antonio, where he lives with his wife and two sons.

G. Miki Hayden: How does a writer learn to actually write?
Rick Riordan: Creative writing classes or books about writ-

ing can offer you tips and insights, perhaps even inspire you to keep going. But they can't really teach you to write. You have to roll up your sleeves and get on the word processor— every day, no excuses. And you have to force yourself to produce, not just endlessly polish the same few pages. Secondarily, writers learn to write by reading. I don't subscribe to the theory that you shouldn't read while you're trying to write for fear that you'll end up sounding like that author. You have to trust that your own voice is strong enough to come through. By reading good authors, you learn structure. You learn about voice and style and effective plotting. You also learn what the competition is up to!

GMH: Can you give aspiring mystery writers some specific clues as to what to watch for regarding technique?

RR: The best course I ever took to help my own writing was a graduate level grammar course for teachers, designed to present the structure of English from a teacher's point of view. We can all normally pick out a written passage that sounds wrong, but how do you explain what's wrong with it? How do you help a student fix the writing? I've come to realize since taking that class that most of the manuscripts publishers reject just aren't technically competent. The spelling may be okay, and the punctuation may be right, but the style is weak. The sentence structure is ineffective. My best tip in terms of technique is to raise your own awareness of sentence composition, whether with the help of a good book on style or a grammar class at your local college. The effort will pay off.

GMH: How about getting an agent?

RR: Don't contact an agent prematurely. Your manuscript must be finished, and it must be as good as you can possibly make it. Then and only then, spend an afternoon at the reference desk of your local library, looking through *The Literary Marketplace*, or a similar guide to agents. Think big for your first queries—target twenty agents who seem to handle the sort of work you do. Send them each a one-page letter describing your book and offering to send them sample chapters. Be courteous and professional. Agents and publishers appreciate an author who takes a businesslike approach.

GMH: What's the most important thing a mystery writer should do to promote?

RR: Promotion is every bit as essential to the success of your work as the actual writing. Apply yourself to PR with the same diligence and energy. Meet the booksellers in your area. Sign books whenever and wherever you get the chance. Don't get crushed if no one comes to a signing—that's not the point of a signing, anyway. The publicity and visibility you generate at that store before and after is much more important than the event itself. Be positive, excited, and optimistic about what you're doing. Treat your readers with respect. After all, they have the final say in your success.

Seymour Shubin

His Killers Aren't Just Crazy—They're *Real*

Seymour Shubin is one writer who doesn't simply use a villain as a device; the murders in his books aren't merely an excuse for detection. As an author, Shubin wants to know why, why has this terrible crime occurred? Or, more accurately, he wants to show his readers what is behind the grim occurrences.

The author of 12 published crime fiction novels, many short stories, and hundreds of journalistic articles, Shubin continues to write and publish. His *The Good and the Dead* (Write Way), *The Captain* and *Anyone's My Name* (both Creative Arts Books) are currently in print, but his impressive backlist, such as *Fury's Children* and *My Face Among Strangers*, are well worth seeking out. Shubin is a writer's writer and a true professional.

G. Miki Hayden: You were a journalist. What drove you to fiction?

Seymour Shubin: Actually, I wrote fiction long before I even thought of becoming a journalist—beginning at about age 15 (and poetry even before that). Though I had a lot of other qualms, I had absolutely none about submitting my stories to national magazines. They all came back, of course, until one was taken by a syndicate when I was about 18, and then the legendary *Story Magazine* took one some time after that. The latter resulted in my getting an agent.

GMH: Your central figures are usually psychologically tormented. Why have you chosen this offbeat approach?

SS: I think, more accurately, that it chooses me. Perhaps at least part of this came from my past experience as a writer of true detective stories, when I would often accompany police on raids and surveillances, and also wrote many first-person stories from the criminal's point of view. I encountered the most ordinary looking people who had committed the most horrendous crimes. It didn't take much for me to realize what a narrow line it was to cross between right and crime. I also must have carried my own sense of latent guilt that led many reviewers of my first novel in particular, *Anyone's My Name*, to write that its underlying theme was "There but for the grace of God . . . " It's something I do believe.

GMH: The Captain earned you a lot of kudos, including a coveted Edgar nomination. Did that change your life?

SS: The major thing it did was help get *The Captain* reissued as a trade paperback, today, years later. Part of the reason was that the book never quite died in the sense that I kept hearing from people about it over the years. But it was also a source of stress until it was originally published. *The Captain* was turned down by many publishers and agents, who didn't think an "old" protagonist was commercial enough.

GMH: The background in your books is always so authentic. What research goes into a book like *The Captain*?

SS: *The Captain* was a special book in that a lot of research went into it—even before I knew there would be such a novel. For one thing, my wife had worked in the office of a nursing home. For another, as a writer and former editor of a journal for psychiatrics, I had done a lot of writing about the elderly. I also had known a detective captain, deceased, many of whose attributes I either used or imagined. So when I finally did think of *The Captain*, the research was essentially done.

As far as research in general goes, I actually do very little. Part of the reason may be that I did so much research as a freelance journalist that I don't feel like plunging into it again. But the most important reason is that I use bits and fragments of what I know, and take off from there. And wherever possible, I use fictional settings—or fictional parts of real settings—so that if I want to put a lake in the middle of it, I can.

GMH: You've had a lot of success with short stories. What made you go in that direction?

SS: As I've mentioned, I began writing short stories before I attempted a novel. What I like about the short mystery is that these stories are not—quote *not*—slices of life. I like a story with a beginning, middle—and you know what else—a good ending. But I generally don't write stories that are mysteries in the traditional sense. They're usually stories about a crime, with a punch at the finish.

GMH: What is your approach to writing a novel? How long does it take you?

SS: They used to take me about a year. But while writing *The Captain*, which was the fourth of my twelve novels, I came up with a method that really released me. I write the first draft without looking back, and that involves mistakes and accidental changes of names and what-have-you. So I don't edit myself as I go along. Once I have it down, I then do the rewriting—but now, at least, I have something of substance to work on. I would say it takes me about six months to complete a book.

GMH: How does a writer learn to actually write?

SS: We learn from experimentation, even though at the beginning this may lead to failure after failure. We learn by permitting ourselves to *not* be super-perfect in our writing. I would advise new writers not to edit themselves on a first draft. This is especially true of a long work, a book, where many people edit themselves into paralysis, and then drop the whole thing. Once you have something down, no matter how badly written or mistake-riddled, it's something real to be changed and polished. Merciless self-criticism can kill what we want to create.

In talking to writers' groups, I'm always surprised by the number of people who say they're afraid to send anything out to magazines or book publishers. To me, it's as though they're afraid an editor will hold a rejection against them. Or maybe they themselves can't handle rejection. If so, what a wrong business they're in. I look on it like trying to train a horse in a barn without letting him out to race.

GMH: Can you give aspiring mystery writers some specific clues as to what to watch for regarding technique?
SS: Nothing is more important in a mystery novel than pace. And nothing is more deadly than the lack of it. So, how do you maintain a novel's pace? Well, one small but obvious way is through the use of an occasional question that quickly submerges the reader into the conflicts and suspense of the story—for instance: Why does he kill only in the rain?

One of the things you should be on the alert for are patches of your writing that literally stop the flow of the action like a heavy foot on the brake. For example, does the description you're using, say of the sun setting on the hills, interrupt your story? Well, instead of pausing to describe a scene, you might consider "seeing" it through the eyes and thoughts of the person involved, perhaps as he or she is running or is about to kill someone. In other words, make the description part of the flow of the story. The same is true of dialogue. Too much extraneous dialogue might show facets of your knowledge, but be aware that in a novice's hands superfluous speech can also be a "killer." Think of dialogue as part of the action.

As to the action itself, the aspiring mystery writer won't make a mistake by "cutting to the chase" as quickly as possible. Let's say you want your protagonist to visit a certain apartment. Is it really necessary that you show him or her driving there? If anything of interest happens on the ride, you might want to start off with the protagonist at the apartment door (where we know *something* is going to happen) and thinking back to what has already occurred.

GMH: How about getting an agent?

SS: I've long thought that the easiest way to make a million dollars is to start off with a million. And I think the easiest way to get an agent is not to need one. Having said that, here are a few basics to approaching an agent. One, have a complete manuscript to offer. Two, don't send it. Not yet. Look for those expressing an interest in mysteries, and then write to just one at a time—best with a self-addressed, stamped envelope. Here, it's a matter of selling yourself and your book to the point where the agent will ask to see at least a few chapters. But agents can take months to answer. My suggestion is to send a polite query letter after about a month, and if you still don't hear, write to another one.

I have sold several novels without an agent—about which you might be thinking, "Yeah but you already had a publishing history." While that's so, it's *always* an adventure to sell a book on your own. But what's more pertinent here, I know several first-time authors who sold books without an agent. Go to reference books to compile a list of publishers that not only put out mysteries but don't specify that they only accept submissions from agents. And be sure not to overlook the many small presses. Once again, don't just send out your manuscript, even accompanied by the most selling letter. Send the letter first—and make sure it's addressed to a specific editor (you can find this in the references or by phone) and not simply to the company name. Bear in mind that one rejection is not the death knoll for a book. Nor is thirty, or, necessarily, fifty.

Now here's a "problem" I only wish on you. What to do when you get a contract? First, rejoice. Second, read it. Then you might want to go to the list of agents again—this time you're a much easier "sell." If not, talk to your lawyer (if he knows anything about book contracts). If still no, check your library for reference books that include model contracts. And you might also call on the Authors Guild in New York City, to point the way for advice.

GMH: What's the most important thing a mystery writer should do to promote?

SS: Assuming that your publisher is going to do such things as notify talk-shows and feature editors (at least in your community) about your upcoming novel, the key thing to do—shortly before the book is published—is introduce yourself to book store managers and/or other personnel. Tell them you're available for readings and signings. Some bookstores have started "mystery clubs" whose members meet monthly, with authors as speakers. If a store doesn't have a club, suggest that the manager start one.

But be prepared that this may sound easier than it really

is. Unless you live in a community where a novelist is an instant celebrity, most bookstore people have met more than a few authors before you. Now, some personnel are an immediate delight; they're happy just to shake you hand and will talk on and on with you. But then there are others who look elsewhere as you talk. Yet even these people can be eased down by your approach. And then there are those personnel who fall somewhere in the middle, and soon turn into a pleasure to be with.

Most writers don't find it easy to put on what I call a "salesman's hat." After all, if we wanted to be salesmen we wouldn't go into writing. But then again, if we didn't want our books out there to be read, most of us would never have gone through all the hurdles and sweat and disappointment, to reach the point where we finally need that "hat."

Kris Neri

An Author With a Lot of Revenge on Her Mind

Kris Neri's mystery, *Revenge of the Gypsy Queen*, was only in print for one short week when the novel, featuring a mystery author intent on doing duty as an amateur P.I., was chosen as a Detective Book Club monthly selection. The pick was a great honor for any mystery, much less a first effort from a smaller press (Rainbow Books). Eventually, *Revenge* was nominated for Agatha, Anthony, and Macavity awards for best first mystery—an incredible response.

Neri's Tracy Eaton originally appeared in a story called "L.A. Justice," which was published in the anthology *Murder by Thirteen* (Intrigue Press), and which won a Derringer award from the Short Mystery Fiction Society in 1998. Neri's second novel, *Dem Bones' Revenge*, also starring Tracey Eaton, came out in Fall 2000.

G. Miki Hayden: How did you learn to actually write?

Kris Neri: My first useful lessons in writing came during my freshman comp class in college. I lucked out with an exceptionally creative instructor. She encouraged us to know the grammatical rules, but to use them as tools, rather than being slaves to them. We were told to write for the effect we wanted to achieve. If we did break a grammatical rule, we had to identify that parenthetically so she knew we weren't simply making a mistake. But we were judged on the effectiveness and power of the writing. My instructor told me to write the way I speak, the way I want readers to experience my thoughts. The idea that I should be shooting for that objective hit me like a thunderbolt. I began to put more of myself on the page, beginning a process that continues to this day.

GMH: Can you give aspiring mystery writers some specific clues as to what to watch for regarding technique?

KN: Newer writers tend to start their books too far in the past. They also often give too much information about the background of characters and/or the history of relationships between the characters, and they provide that background too early in the book. Where in the story should a book start? That's always the writer's choice, but, ideally, it shouldn't be too far before the discovery of the crime, or at least, whatever will trigger the crime. Back story should be doled out in such a way that it creates more questions in the reader's mind. The author should use background to intrigue the reader, to make the reader keep reading.

Often, too, new writers create scenes in which the characters simply stand around talking. It's essential that characters be grounded in well-textured places and spaces, and that they interact with the world around them. To capture a sense of place, I've found it helpful to focus on that place early in the story-planning process. The setting will automatically begin to impact the plot and will become thoroughly integrated into the story. Some new writers establish their settings well, but then seem to forget about them once the story takes off. How enjoyable would a stage play be if the set and lighting were phased out as the play progressed? The setting must remain a presence throughout the book. And the characters must continue to interact with the background and handle the props the background provides. When you make the setting an important part of your book, you also show us more about the characters who inhabit those spaces, and make them more alive for us.

GMH: How about getting an agent?

KN: Writers need to introduce themselves with a topnotch query letter that opens with a hook—the intriguing high concept of your book, even the opening line, if it's a grabber. Then go on with a short, interesting description of the story. Make the description read like a book jacket blurb. But don't include the ending in your query—make them want to read the whole manuscript. Indicate the kind of book you've written and give a word count. But don't classify the story too narrowly within a subgenre. Relate your work to the books of prominent authors whose writings share some similarities with yours, saying, "It might appeal to the readers of X, Y, or Z." If you have any writing credits, describe them in their best light. But never apologize if this is your first written project. If your background or career contributed to the writing of this book, that's valuable as a credit. End with a strong closing, and thank that person for considering the book. "I hope you like it" sounds too unsure.

A query should always be addressed to a person, not an agency or publishing company. If you don't know the contact's name, call and ask. And always address that individual as Mr. or Ms. until s/he uses your first name. The tone should be polite and courteous as well as professional and confident. If you can capture the attitude of the book in your query, that's wonderful. Spelling and grammar mistakes will count against you. And if you're preparing a number of queries at one time, make sure you put the right letter into the right envelope!

GMH: What's the most important thing a mystery writer should do to promote?

KN: I'd have to say it would be making sure there were sufficient reviews of the book. Readers give far more weight to reviews than they do to the author's own self-serving promotion. Some publishers don't send review copies, or only send a few. But most will allow the author to supplement that number at his own expense. The bigger review outlets will only read advanced copies well before publication, and those should come from the publisher. But many Internet review sites will read a completed book, even after publication. If a publisher won't support this effort, a wise author buys his own books and sees that they get into the right hands.

A new author must also make the independent mystery booksellers aware of the book that's about to debut. If a book receives outstanding reviews in all the big review outlets, the mystery bookstore owners will know about it. But no author can count on that happening, especially not an author from a smaller house, or an author whose publisher didn't choose to send review copies or sent very few. Labels for all the relevant bookstores can be purchased inexpensively from the ClueLass website (Cluelass.com). Send a prepublication informational package to all the stores. Not only does it make the bookseller more likely to order that book, it gives her the information she needs to hand sell it. Some publishers send advance copies of the book to all the independent mystery booksellers. But many authors make up their own galleys for booksellers, especially for those in their own geographical area. A bookseller who is excited about a new book is going to sell more of them.

8

Under Interrogation

————— A Final Deposition —————

Just when I thought I could rest my case, the judge . . . er, editor . . . issued an . . . uhum, stay . . . After sitting down for a grilling under the lights, I now submit to you, the ultimate jury, the final transcript that resulted—some tough questions asked by writers I've critiqued over the years. While each question pertains to an indiviual's specific work, I feel the lessons here are universal.

The cozies I looked at recently were all in first person. Is it better to write in first than third?

Either first or third works equally well—depending on what you're comfortable with and what you feel best suits the story. People make a bit of a deal about the difference, but I see virtually no major advantage to one over the other. Both forms sell and both are admired by readers of every subgenre. I have never heard an editor express a preference for either first or third person and I have asked a few what they are looking for.

That said, I find greater latitude in creating a character in third person. More can be described from outside the character, as well as attributed to him or her in an impersonal manner. Third person also avoids forcing the presumption onto the reader that the "I" of the protagonist is the author's own voice. This mental association of the "I" with the author can cause those finding the narrator a bit of a lamebrain to become rather annoyed at you, the mere writer. But this is minor, because those same traits will come through, anyway, and the author will often be "blamed" for the character's failings.

Can I write a prologue in third person and then convert to first person for the rest of the novel? Otherwise, when can I change the point of view (POV)? I'm confused.

By all means write a sort of prologue, even if you don't call it that, in third person, then switch to the main body of the story in first person. I say "even if you don't call it that" because some readers and editors hate or fear that thing called "the prologue." They have unbending prejudices against the device and strict rules for limiting it. Therefore, you might want to make the prologue your first scene in chapter one, instead.

One of the worst things you can do is switch POV within a scene. You can change POV when you go on to a new scene, however. You might try to tell me that J. D. Robb (Nora Roberts in her mystery guise) interrupts her scenes with the parking meter's POV, but how Nora Roberts writes doesn't matter in any case. She can and you can't. That's because she is a proven bestseller.

When you are in your character's head, remember, you can't know anything the character himself doesn't know. You can't know why the other person does something and you have to make sure that a guess about what that character feels is merely the POV character's guess.

Short stories are usually, but not always, from a single POV. In a novel, that depends. Some are from one POV and some are from many points of view. These are different styles intended to achieve different goals. The typical mystery is written in a simple way from a single protagonist's POV. However, even a simple mystery can have scenes from other points of view—although this must create some type of a pattern, even an irregular one. You can't have only one scene in the book from a second POV.

While you may have other POV scenes in order to relate material that is needed for your story, there must be a clear purpose to using this technique. You might want to tell something before the protagonist discovers the information, for instance, or relate facts that the protagonist will never learn. Be aware when a different POV scene could simply be handled by that person coming to the protagonist or being interviewed by the protagonist and giving the information directly. You may or may not then want the different POV.

What do you mean when you talk about going back to the work and "layering in" information?

Often writers have not provided various elements in their original draft and have to return and layer them in—setting, internal dialogue, sensory information—any of those details that transmits a "coating" of meaning to the reader. If we were archeologists of the word, digging down into someone's story, we, hopefully, could uncover each stratum and find a marvelous, striking abundance of rich expressiveness. The ideal is to be able to sketch in all layers in one draft and then just go back a couple of times to polish the wording. But returning to fill in the layers is not a terrible way to approach the need for added coloration. So long as the layers get laid down and then convey many shades of significance, the outcome is as prescribed.

Since I'm writing a cozy, not a thriller, can I start off a bit slower?

Initial pacing for cozies, in my opinion, should be just as fast as for thrillers. The reasoning for this is actually the same in both cases. The person you want to catch right off the bat is the editor, who reads about 20 of these submissions per day. Well, no one can read 20 a day. . . . Exactly right. She doesn't *read* 20 manuscripts, although she might go through 20. If you don't catch her on the fly, as it were, you don't catch her at all and she could care less. No matter the sub-genre, always start strong. Then go back and muse and develop all you like. Well, not all you like, because every novel has to continue to move forward and not lag too badly.

I haven't been able to sell my romantic suspense. Do you think I could rework this as a mystery?

In mystery, the romance, if you have it, probably should be light, already established, or come at the end after the two have been at odds. The main thing is for the novel to focus on the investigation or case and for the female protagonist not to be dependent on the male to solve the mystery. Any romance is a sidebar. Mystery readers want the female investigator—whether an amateur or not—to be on her own, although she may also have subordinate helpers or sometimes be an equal partner. Your romantic suspense wouldn't work for mystery, if she's only a tagalong.

What if I have my villain under contract to the Egyptian government to steal back the artifacts?

Having the Egyptians pay him to commit a crime bothers me quite a bit, because that's book logic. My personal taste is against book logic and toward real-life reasoning since, for me, the trappings of authenticity sit easier in a novel. Likely, in the world we all generally occupy, the government of Egypt would go through legal channels to reclaim the country's treasures—beginning with diplomatic protests and various types of political maneuverings. If, after reading an article about the controversy, your villain simply imagines that he can sell the art back to the Egyptians, that might jibe with the character structure of a genuinely dumb criminal. But that's my own preference. A lot of mystery writers write book logic solely and are extremely popular and quite well paid.

Does my novel's pacing seem okay so far?

You've built up quite a lot of mystery here. Now, believe it or not, you need to back off from setting the puzzle. Return to the protagonist's home life and have her fuss over the children—since they're integral to the investigation. You need some plateau for a couple of chapters, that's just what I think. You've brought the story to a boil, so you can reduce the heat and let the plot simmer. Unfortunately the analogy doesn't play out because in cooking you don't have to turn the heat up again—oh well.

Not all novels will need the leveling off after a build. Some will be nonstop action, like the movie, *The Fugitive*. But yours is not that type of book. You have a conundrum here that the protagonist—and we as the readers—need to consider for a while. We don't need more mystery thrown at us right now.

What do you mean when you tell me the "rhythm" or "pacing" is wrong?

As a small press editor said to me today, "Writers have to develop an inner 'ear.' Too often stories don't work because the rhythm is off."

To me, this applies not only to each sentence—which the statement very much also concerns—but to the other elements as well—the rhythm of what should be said and when. Timing is everything. Much of the author's job is not only telling the story, but having the judgment to express the tale in correct sequences and in the proper "voice."

How is this internal sensing brought into being? Slowly, over time, through both reading and writing. When someone practices a craft over a period of years, this second sense comes into existence. You already have part of that feel for how a story is dramatized. Keep working and the faculty will inevitably deepen.

Can I have an ambiguous ending? I'm planning a series that picks up where this novel leaves off.

The ending of a novel doesn't have to offer absolute closure. The degree to which you tie up loose ends depends on the thematic focus of the story. I don't, myself, always end with an arrest, if my point has been more character than plot. I enjoy a certain amount of real-life uncertainty. On the other hand, some stories require a well-defined end and the readers deserve that. Certainly you can't make them buy another book to discover the finale of the one they have purchased and are reading now. They not only won't pick up the next book, they will be angry and suggest that no one buy this one.

What should happen by the end of any novel? Something might change—either the situation or the character, or often both. Or neither may change, if that is the point of the story—that is, the author might express the view that these characters don't/won't change and, despite some peak event, their little world is either stagnant or secure (depending on how the author sees that element). In other words, the author creates the parameters in order to express some POV about the world.

But whatever the message, this must be conveyed via some sort of conclusion which leaves the reader satisfied that at least he or she comprehends the writer's intent. Most frequently, mysteries close with the crime being solved and the bad person disposed of in a proper way, but room exists for another type of ending, such as on Law & Order, where from time to time the criminal is judged "not guilty" by an unsophisticated jury—and no more can be done.

What do you mean when you say I have to "tighten" my writing?

When creating your fiction, you need to think about every word you set down—perhaps not when you first write the piece, but on the several re-drafts it's really a must. When you write, or re-write, a sentence, try to imagine how you could express the idea using fewer words with greater impact each. What if you had to pay five cents for every word you wrote and kept? You'd be a lot more careful with each one, right?

Don't use words that have no value. And don't use words that are extraneous. For instance, *I stood up and offered her my hand* can be *I stood and offered her my hand*. I notice that you use prepositions with verbs when they aren't necessary. This is a fairly common writer's flaw, but you do this repeatedly, so watch for and avoid that type of excess.

I wrote some sections that I really like, but you told me to cut them. How come?

Focus on the "why" of the scene and write to the why. Every scene has a reason for being in the novel and you must stick to the reason for its existence and not wander. That will mean leaving out unimportant portions. Then, when you are concentrated on a topic related to the main concern, you can go to town in presenting your details.

Each scene should do only what it's supposed to do and no more . . . There are no surprises in getting someone into an ambulance and the details should not be part of the storyline. Moreover, do not bother to describe a character at length who will not appear later in the book.

How do you know if you are simply yammering about something that isn't essential? Even if you don't have the plot nailed down, you do know what the focus of your book will be—or you should. The scenes and their contents have to be directed toward the focus and be absolutely necessary to carrying through the entire novel. Where segments are not integral to the central focus, chuck the writing. Be strict with yourself, not self-indulgent

Any novel might need a setup scene that appears to not be connected with the murder, of course. Such a scene might be required despite not being related to the mystery per se. A political thriller, for instance, might need some initial scenes to establish the terrifying situation. While the first scene may well set the time bomb ticking, scene two might show the protagonist oblivious to the horror to come.

Why do you say this scene has to be cut?

The "scene" is more than 4,000 words long. A novel of this type—a contemporary series mystery—should probably clock in at 65,000 words—70,000, tops. That means you will have about 16 or 17 scenes in this book at 4,000 words each—20 scenes if you write some of them lean. Say the average number of scenes per chapter in a mystery of this type counts out at three. Do you think you'll complete your story arc by the end?

No one has shorter scene and chapter lengths than Mary Higgins Clark as I recall. She does okay with that, I've heard. Always with questions of this kind, you can go to the bookstore and leaf through books similar to yours to determine appropriateness. If nothing seems to be the same as yours and yet what you have chosen feels right to you, ignore the models—but cautiously and without arrogance.

You said my dialogue is too narrative and not natural. How can I prevent that?

The author shouldn't jam a lot of narrative—the back story or other details—into the dialogue. Listen to real speech and try to reproduce the essence, while smoothing out the stops and starts. Moreover, I think you would do better in taking some of the narrative outside the quotes. Add most of those details inside the character's internal POV material. Don't have her say, *I thought Belinda would come to my rescue.* Instead, declare: *She had expected Belinda to come to her rescue during the discussion with John.*

Let's *see* as well as hear during the dialogue, too. What are the characters physically doing? Is the POV character taking notes? Staring out the window? Fill in the scene. Conversation between two people doesn't happen in limbo, with nothing else going on.

Add the emotional texture to the dialogue as well. *Kate's voice vibrated with a tone of edgy weariness . . .*

Why shouldn't I have a phonetic representation of the sound fffft slllrrrg? I have seen that type of thing elsewhere.

I personally prefer to see a verbal representation of sound because that's what we do in writing—verbally represent—*the telephone rang*. Also, recognize that the first thing which happens in reading is that the reader's eyes fall on the page. Does the page itself appear inviting, or does the arrangement seem confusing? How well does the visual sense feeding the brain allow interpretation of something such as *fffft slllrrrg*? To me, the words signal "oh oh, this is something I'm not going to understand and want to skim over." As Elmore Leonard is often quoted as saying, "Leave out the parts that the readers skip anyway."

Why don't you like my male character? I do.

The internal voice of your male character is too angry. Whether or not he's justified in his complaints, we won't be attracted to someone who is so sour. Your reporter, however, has a decently believable and pleasant inner voice. If she gets involved with the cop, I'm sending her to be on *Oprah* so she can get rid of the toxic people in her life.

I'm sure he's really a kind and decent guy underneath, but I don't have patience for his overt discontent and crabby attitude. While this type of characterization has worked for Sipowitz on *NYPD Blue*, that's because he has always been offset by sweet, soft-spoken, and intelligent partners. And, of course, we do see Andy's kindness and caring, when push comes to shove.

We can create characters who aren't mainstream nice, but we have to tread a careful line and not show their worst qualities up front and unmitigated, unless they also display some unusual and arresting personality element that immediately intrigues us.

How do I develop a character?

One can develop a character to a great degree via internal thought and via action. I would also emphasize description of personality per se. *Known in town as a stingy son-of-a-gun, Billy Ray was not the type of guy to be that generous for no reason at all. What was he hiding? Or, Cheryl knew she had a reputation for biting people's heads off at the least provocation and usually tried to curb herself, but this time, she didn't really care . . .* That blatant "tell, don't show" (so sue me) develops character.

The advice often given is to give the character a gimmick, a head for figures or a physical tick. We're also told to provide a physical description, often indirectly. *She looked in the mirror and saw a reasonably attractive, five foot six blonde in her 20s.* Actually, that's fine if she's the one with a head for figures and the limp, the combination of which make her more interesting. Too generic a description and she's a boring disappointment.

You also need to integrate elements of thoughts and feelings. Always. You cannot have prose without giving us an inkling of what is going on inside your character's minds and emotions. You might say, *he frowned,* and we get the idea, or you can give his thoughts directly. *Something smelled fishy here. Tommy was lying.*

What do you mean by saying, "Be concrete"?

Words are representations, but of something that exists. You need to be very exact in reproducing reality. You need to be the readers' eyes and ears. Don't expect readers to figure things out—you have to present a one-for-one correspondence with the image/world you are creating. Don't say *she took the powder with her.* Explain that *she put the powder in an old vitamin bottle and stuffed the container in her purse.* Ground the words in reality. This will provide much greater effect. Tie everything of this sort down to specifics. Leave nothing vague, since we form a visual representation from what you write.

I thought writing is supposed to be innovative and unique. You told me the way I phrased something "is not the way this is usually said." What's wrong with that?

Many phrases are generally spoken and written in a certain way and that's the way we expect to hear or read them. You do not need to diverge from that as a novelist—except in those places where you choose a different use for emphasis or make a stylistic selection. Most of the time you are well advised to state the words in the traditional way. Doing otherwise puts the reader on the alert that something special is going on. If nothing out of the ordinary is happening, this is a false signal. Most often when I find these unusual phrasings, the writer simply doesn't know the typical way the comment is made. Sometimes, the writer has heard the saying wrongly and the misstatement becomes a howler—a funny to the more literate.

How should I handle time lapses?

How you deal with time depends on the needs of the story, but you don't have to literally walk steplock with your protagonist. You can start new scenes by skipping some space, which indicates a lapse of time. Or you can present a time lapse through your wording. You don't have to accompany the characters walking out to the car, but you can show him opening the car door for her and our mind's eye will fill in the gaps—they walked out to the car, obviously. You can also start sections with *After dinner* ... Or *On Tuesday* ... which will orient us as to *when.*

I have a problem writing because I can't type that fast.

Think of your pace at the keyboard as giving you time to consider your words. To tell you the truth, I take breaks every few minutes and form sentences on my way to the refrigerator, etc.—it works out fine. Just type away at your own speed and never mind any sense of frustration. Concentrate on the words and the ideas. . . .

How do I write a red herring into my mystery?

You have mentioned the legendary "red herring" with a sense of "when I find out about *that* ...."—as if tossing in a misleading clue were the key to writing this form of fiction. Sorry to tell you, but the red herring isn't actually the grand essential. The primary key, if there is one, is to maintain the focus and the intensity of the protagonist's search. We have to know that the character is fixated on this situation and that the barriers to its solution are almost insurmountable— although there also has to be continual movement in solving whatever the dilemma is.

I know you are thinking that writing crime fiction requires a slightly unfathomable sleight of hand, but honestly, at base, it doesn't. While there are artful ways of building a mystery, these novels can be very different from one another in the approaches used. What succeeds is pretty much unique in every instance. As I've noted before, some crime fiction even begins with the disclosure of the killer.

In regard to the red herring specifically and to "planting" these, this is done merely by intending to mislead the reader. You don't have to even know the killer to do this. You, as the author, can yourself suspect every character—in fact, you should. Even knowing who the killer is, you, in the protagonist's place, must suspect everyone. Therefore, certain innocent actions will always seem suspicious to the investigator and can be played for effect. It's simply that easy. Naturally, as the author, you will make sure that certain events look especially shady.

You must, however, in the end, have an explanation for every event that appeared peculiar. *(Oh, I took the key because I thought it was the key to the lady's room. Sorry.)* Not too long ago, I read a book by a somewhat successful mystery author. The book was full of every device and red herring possible. By the time the conclusion was offered, the author could not explain half of the chaos she had created, so she never even tried. I won't read (review) another of hers. She cheated badly. Don't cheat—too much. You will have to explain everything eventually. So when you mislead (write in a red herring), make sure you can clarify the facts later on.

Why can't I begin my mystery with some flashbacks?

You don't want to overload the beginning with the back story. Are you sure you're opening at the right point? You might prefer to open earlier and then cut forward instead of going back. Flashbacks should be used cautiously as they can confuse the reader and certainly disrupt the normal sequence of events. My sense of things is that one starts the mystery and then goes on. You don't go back unless you need to toward the end to clarify a point—but even then, that is generally not done by means of a flashback.

Why do you call my opening "crowded"?

You have a great deal to say and you're trying to fit it all in at once. The material is interesting and you do have a hook at the start, but the hook, which is strong, is buried, so you have to unbury it. You also have to remember that you have a whole book ahead of you and you can dole out your wonderfully rich material in measured doses. Believe me, I am going to want to read your book, so just slow down. I'll stay with you. You don't have to tell everything at one time. You have me with the hook, now reel me in.

How should I go forward with the plotting?

The process of plotting involves knowing more than your characters do, as well as knowing what type of story you are writing and what you want to accomplish in terms of structure. Some structures are very complex and contain many threads; some are relatively straightforward and involve one crime and its solution with, perhaps, one subplot. Decide on a subgenre and a general organization for the book. Then concentrate on what the protagonists feel and what the goal of the criminal is (if you know it) versus the good guy's objective in regard to the crime.

The plot follows the characters—that's absolutely what happens. In fact, you intend something for a scene and the darn characters twist it all out of shape. But is that really so bad? The plot is simply one element in the novel and is not sacrosanct.

I've outlined my plot, but if I write it the way I outlined it, the novel will be over in about ten thousand words. How do I lengthen this?

I think what you're saying is that you don't know how to fill in between major plot points. You can do that with subplots and by introducing new characters. This is the type of endeavor that you just have to accomplish by feel alone. As you're writing, you will get the sense that something is bogging down—or being revealed too quickly. At that point you go into problem-solving mode.

What I have been hearing from you is that your problem-solving mode isn't in good working order. It should be, because the mind is the most wonderful and creative computer possible. Something in you knows what will shore up the plot—or what will be a terrific, perfect twist. Just keep working on the thinking part. I like to plot while walking or exercising. I find my mind works well and without stress at those times. Maybe for you, an idea will pop up in the morning or while you are eating a meal or watching TV.

I hate to say it, but what happens next almost doesn't matter, so long as the focus of the novel is maintained. I was watching North by Northwest the other night, a great example of a ridiculous plot! But what a movie!!! Focus/barrier and movement—that's how the Hitchcock-developed story flows.

You shouldn't have to drop a project because you can't forward the plot. (Although this happens.) Once I was quite deeply into a novel and then couldn't think of the next event to come. So I had my characters wander the desert in frustration—my frustration. And, you know what? That worked superbly. Writing was agonizing for me while I was trying to get through my plot block, but that "getting nowhere" portion was perfect for the story. Sadly, that technique can't be used for every mystery you write, but keep reaching for the answer.

My romantic suspense doesn't seem suspenseful. Should I re-write the plot?

Suspense, frankly, is hard to maintain. How many suspense novels have you read where your heart was actually beating a little faster and you were on the edge of your seat? Not many, I'd bet.

As for re-plotting to add the suspense—I don't think so. The suspense is not actually in the plot. The suspense is in our attachment to the character and the continual sense of foreboding that you place in the words. Even during the romantic scenes, you have to break away, slightly, with a phrase or a paragraph to insert the concern. Do not go pages at a time without that fear or the reader will think, "The character's not worried, so why should I be?" That's it. Just keep reminding them.

What does literary mean?

Literary fiction is defined as "serious" and individualistic, demonstrating deeper meaning. But generally, today, literature will be everything with the exception of specific-genre writing: science fiction, mystery, romance, and cross-genre. Genre stories and novels can also be literary, however. That means they are less formulaic. In novels, the imprints that publish what they call literary try to issue those literary books that they consider to be on the commercial side—meaning they hope those books will have a wider appeal than merely experimental or intellectual novels.

I met two editors at a conference who asked to see my mystery. Can I send this without a summary? I'm afraid a summary might allow them to reject some story line they don't like.

The standard submission format is to include a summary, even with a full manuscript. If, however, you choose not to send the summary, you might view that as testing a strategy. In making two submissions, you could send one with a summary and one without, then compare the results. I'd advise always trying tests of that type. In sending multiple queries, use a couple of different query letter formats and track which one gets better responses.

Should I tell the editors that this is a simultaneous submission? Or should I just submit one at a time?

The official line is to not submit simultaneously. Yet agents make more than one submission at a time, so, in my view, an individual has the same freedom to send to all the publishers at once. If you submit yourself, you will receive a response in any potential time frame, from two weeks to two years. If you were to submit one manuscript at a time, how long would you wait before sending the second manuscript? You wouldn't wait two years. So why would you delay the second submission to begin with? You feel that you have something to lose. You don't. If the editor wants the book, she wants the book. If she doesn't, she doesn't.

I would certainly not mention, however, that I am making simultaneous submissions. That is a near-guarantee that you will receive a rejection, since the editors look for any excuse to get a manuscript off their desks. This is all my own opinion, formed after a number of years of observing the submissions process. A lot of what goes on here is a psychological game. Did I mention that no legalities are involved? This is your property that you are selling and our system of economic life is blessed capitalism. Make the most of it. Be as aggressive as you need to be to sell your work. Don't let anyone intimidate you.

Should I submit my short story to more than one market at the same time? I'm afraid to anger any one editor.

My personal belief, which I'm sure many people in this business would debate strenuously (they have), is that editors are too unreliable to allow them an exclusive look at a good story—despite their guidelines. If, however, you are worried about alienating a particular publication or two, ones that you want to target forevermore, you can submit on an exclusive basis to your A list and then try simultaneous submissions to your B list.

I have written a number of short stories. Might I be able to sell an anthology of my own work? Should I simply self-publish an anthology?

No publisher will have interest in a short story compilation unless the author is fairly well known. If the plan is to self-publish, then the problem will be the same as with all self-publishing ventures—distribution and marketing. By placing your stories in a self-published book, you are losing your first North American rights on material that you might, otherwise, sell to a respected, or at least occasionally read, magazine. You are also missing the opportunity for feedback from editors who read short stories every day. This is a feedback that most relatively new writers need. You must find out what the world has to say about your writing, even if the "comment" is only a form rejection.

My agent suggests that if I sell some short stories to the known mystery magazines, this will help in selling my series. How can I learn to write short stories for the top magazines?

Your agent has a valid point that publication, especially in Ellery Queen and Alfred Hitchcock, will strengthen your position in trying to sell a mystery series. These magazines are tough markets themselves, however.

The short story, of course, will have limited scope, including, setting, characters, time frame, and number of threads. As with a novel, you will have a central conflict that drives the story, meaning two characters, usually, with opposing goals—the criminal and the investigator. If you know your investigator, then think a little bit about what you want in a villain. What crime does your bad person commit—and where? You have the basic frame of the story then, which runs along the lines of pursuit and avoidance, a seeking to know versus a seeking to obfuscate.

The way to find out how to write the short story form is to keep on writing within its parameters. The EQMM and AHMM stories run fairly long. Figure out the average word count and write to length. If you're aiming only for EQMM and AHMM, remember they take very few first-time authors. What will you do if you can't sell to them? Can you then cut and sell to other publications? If you're being practical, you will try to write with multiple markets in mind.

I was told by a friend to have my book edited before submitting to the agents. I never heard of anything like that. Does this make sense?

The publishing houses are doing less editing and want to

buy only very polished books. Therefore, the trend is toward having books pre-edited. Do I think that authors ought to pay for this aspect of the process, in addition to now paying for their own marketing? Not really. On the other hand, I recognize that the publishing environment is very competitive and that writers want to maximize their possibility of acceptance.

Those interested in seeking editorial help should first be aware of a person's credentials and be able to get a sample edit before signing up. By sample edit, I mean at least a couple of paragraphs showing the type of comments that will be made. You should also receive an estimate of cost and will be expected to make some payment upfront.

A complete edit can be very expensive—thousands of dollars rather than hundreds in many cases. Because of this, I would recommend that you get an edit of the first 50 pages, instead of the complete manuscript. From this edit, you may be able to pick up many clues as to your own writing faults, then continue the correction of the entire manuscript on your own. Moreover, if you submit a partial to agents or editors, that means only about 50 pages will be seen first, anyway. If the book doesn't convince on the first 50 pages, you could be stuck with a big editing bill for writing that might never be seen by the outside world. If an editor requests the rest of the book, hopefully you can then get an edit for the remainder of the manuscript. Admittedly, this might be problematic as many editors are booked for several months ahead.

I've had an offer from a small press. Should I sell them my mystery or wait for a better offer?

While we look to the new, small presses to bring diversity to fiction, their distribution is limited in comparison with the mainstream press. Although you can order anything through your local Barnes & Noble—thankfully—the stores do not place routine orders with small press, so copies of their books are not often on the shelves. Still, it's a new day and more and more ordering is done over the Internet, which does not discriminate between the imprints.

People who publish with small press have to work harder than large-press authors, but they can sell somewhat decently. What is decently? Most small press runs—if the press does a run—are 1,500 or so books. Some titles might sell as many as 4,000, considered rather a goodly amount for small press sales. Doesn't sound like much? Try selling that number.

You must be realistic in making your decision of whether or not to go with small press publication. How likely are you to get a better offer? Do you have an agent who has a tremendous track record? Is your book overwhelmingly special? (Not many are.) Have you heard the old saying about "a bird in the hand . . ."?

What is print on demand?

The technology being used by many small presses today is print on demand (POD). Books come off the equipment one at a time and the results generally look good, like an ordinary trade paperback. Unfortunately, the individual books cost a lot to create and the title must be priced accordingly. Therefore, in terms of pricing, they are not always competitive. Moreover, most bookstores won't order these volumes if the publisher has a no-return policy. However, these books can still be sold. A lot of the onus, again, is on the author, who might bring a case of her own books (which she herself has ordered and paid for) to a signing. Also, more of the small press publishers that print by way of POD both take returns and discount to the stores, just as the large publishers do.

What is iUniverse?

iUniverse is a large POD publisher that caters to authors with single titles which they want to self-publish. Some of the authors who publish with them have been pleased with the results, while others have been completely infuriated. Similar operations, such as Xlibris and a number of equivalent enterprises, have provided writers with comparable delights and disappointments. Pros and cons to this type of publishing abound, such as since iUniverse doesn't take returns, these books are a tough sell—even to investment partner Barnes & Noble, which has policies against stocking run-of-the-mill iU books. For the most part, iUniverse profits by selling books to authors and, in that respect, is often charged with being a vanity press. An aggressive author with a fabulous book might sell a few hundred copies, but the odds are not sensational. Still, each to his/her own, and a book in print might be more satisfying to a would-be author than nothing at all.

How can I find the time to write? I have two children.

When I was working and started writing, I was also afraid that I wouldn't find the time. What did happen was I sat down about half an hour a night and wrote anyway, even though I was tired. Pretty soon, I had a novel. Awkwardly formed though it was, I had written one, so I knew I could write another in the same way.

I happened to speak to Mary Higgins Clark on the night of the Edgars awards banquet, when she was named a

Mystery Writers of America Grandmaster. Mary had just signed a $64 million contract for five books. She was widowed at an early age with five little children. Sounds like a made-up story, huh? Every day, she got up early in the morning (in the snow with only a crumb of toast for her breakfast—no, I'm getting carried away) to write before work. I couldn't do that! But Mary did.

One other thing that Mary did, which impresses me—she took the book *Rebecca* by Daphne DuMaurier and wrote out the first and last paragraph of each chapter with a chapter summary. She wanted to know how that book worked.

I am very eager to write and have spent some time doing so, but I have gotten a lot of negative feedback. Should I quit?

I believe that everyone with a desire to learn to write can so do. The desire itself is a strong indicator of potential, in my opinion. I once received a manuscript that was utterly awful—no charm, no real feelings expressed, no setting of the scene. I gave a short critique—just because I was asked. I wasn't disparaging, but I was honest about the flaws. I never heard back from the author and assumed her feelings had been hurt by what I'd said and that she was angry.

A few months later, the scene showed up again—about 90 percent improved over the original. What a joy that was. And I learned that I am not able to know who can benefit from an honest assessment of his or her work.

If I don't know who will succeed, you don't know, either. You have no idea of what your potential is. Therefore, keep writing.

INDEX

Behavior
  of antagonists, 51
  consistency in, 102-103
  and romance, 64
Bellevue Hospital, 182
Berkeley Press, 57
Bierce, Ambrose, 112
Big Red Tequila (Riordan, Rick), 186
Big Sleep, The (Chandler, Raymond), 173
Bijur, Vicky, 171
Biography
  of author, 131, 133
  of characters, 50-51, 103
Biotechnology is Murder (Wyle, Dirk), 13
Bitter Feast, A (Rozan, S.J.), 175
Black Orchid Bookstore, 155
Blyton, Enid, 162
"Boarded Window, The" (Bierce, Ambrose), 112
Book Clubs, 135
Booklist, 142
Books on Tape (*see* Audio Books)
Bookstores
  and mystery clubs, 194
  and ordering, 142, 222
  and promotion, 138, 165, 175, 182, 186, 194, 195
  and research, 62, 81, 117, 209
  and reviews, 142, 199
  and small presses, 4
Borden, Lizzie, 16
Bouchercon (*see* conferences)
Boundary Waters (Krueger, William Kent), 166, 168
Bradbury, Ray, 156
Brainstorming, 100
Brown, Jane Jordan, 167
Browne, D.L., 140
Burke, James Lee, 127
Butcher's Hill (Lippman, Laura), 169
By Reason of Insanity (Hayden, G. Miki), 11, 59

C

Cain, James, 172
Captain, The (Shubin, Seymour), 13, 189, 190-191
Cases (real life), 16, 177-178, 180
Causal relationships (*see also* Relationships), 20
Chandler, Raymond, 8, 31, 157, 173
Chapters, 22-23, 27, 131, 133, 188, 193, 202, 205, 224
  exercises, 23-24
  length of, 22-23, 27, 110, 124-125, 209

Characterization, 43-46, 51, 93, 210
  exercises, 52
  through dialogue, 53, 55
Characters
  and conflict, 31-33
  development of, 26, 40, 43-46, 47-52, 54-56, 82-83, 167, 201, 210-211
  historic figures as, 11-12
  and the McGuffin, 28-29, 31-33
  and mood, 107-108, 217
  relationships between, 20
  secondary, 30-31, 49-51
Charm City (Lippman, Laura), 169
Children's Mysteries, 73, 74, 162
China Trade (Rozan, S.J.), 175
Chinatown History Museum, 177
Chinese Law of Secrecy, 17-18
Christie, Agatha, 7, 10, 43, 157, 162
Clark, Mary Higgins, 14, 134, 209, 223-224
Class (*see* social class or writing class)
Classification (*see* Subgenre)
Clauses
  dependent, 106, 111
  independent, 111
Cliffhanger, 27
Climax (*see also* Story Arc)
  of causal relationships, 20
  of chapters, 23
  and disclosure, 34-35
  mini-, 27, 31, 37, 76
  and pacing, 79-80
ClueFest (*see* Conferences)
ClueLass, 140, 185, 199
"Code Talker" (Hayden, G. Miki), 61
Cold Hit (Fairstein, Linda), 178, 180
Coma (Cook, Robin), 11
Compulsion (Levin, Myer), 16
Computer Brain (*see* intuitive reflex)
Concourse (Rozan, S.J.), 175
Concubine's Tattoo (Rowland, Laura Joh), 63
Conferences
  Bouchercon, 73, 186
  ClueFest, 161
  Left Coast Crime, 186
  Malice Domestic, 164, 170, 186
Conflict
  between characters, 26, 92, 220
  creation of, 26, 192
  exercises, 26
  internal, 148
  and the McGuffin, 28, 31-32

Unholy Orders

Mystery Stories with a Religious Twist

A collection of mystery shorts with religious themes by such acclaimed authors as Anne Perry, G. Miki Hayden, Ralph McInerny, Nancy Pickard, Joyce Christmas, John Lutz, George Chesbro, Margaret Frazer, Kate Charles, Rhys Bowen, and more…

Includes *Agatha, Anthony, McCavity and Derringer* award nominated stories: Widow's Peak, Amish Butter, The Chosen and The Seal of the Confessional

Anne Perry (*The Reverend Collins' Visit*) Irony abounds as a devious jewel thief is methodically exposed by the casual observations of a wry intellectual.

Rochelle Krich (*Widow's Peak*) Ghosts of past misfortune swirl around this enchanting tale of Jewish marriage.

Nancy Pickard (*Speak No Evil*) A self-assured FBI agent's desperate attempt to locate a serial killer leads to a chilling personal encounter with the Devil.

Margaret Frazer (*Volo te habere…*) The bishop of Winchester must settle a question of marriage to expose a killer in this medieval yarn.

G. Miki Hayden (*The Shaman's Song*) An out-of-demand Navajo shaman with his eye on marriage offers his divination skills to clear up a trading post robbery and murder.

Dianne Day (*The Labyrinthine Way*) A priest at an enchanting modern cathedral hypnotizes and captures a dangerous criminal in a gothic labyrinth.

Tom Kreitzberg (*The Charity of a Saint*) A journalist's gentle investigation of a small town miracle in rural England reveals a clever ruse and a quirk of faith.

Rhys Bowen (*The Seal of the Confessional*) Angel or murderer? Forgiveness or revenge? A disturbed repentant seals his fate in the sacrament of penance.

John Lutz (*Dilemma*) A cop faces her first on-the-job moral crisis when she witnesses a priest pick-pocketing a parade crowd.

Joyce Christmas (*The Chosen*) High school girlfriends encounter the extraordinary in a depressed small town.

George Chesbro (*Model Town*) The investigation into a "weeping virgin" uncovers a suspicious trail of tears.

Jacqueline Fiedler (*Amish Butter*) A stranded woman's identity could be the difference between life and death in a nightmarish car ride through Amish country.

Kate Charles (*That Old Eternal Triangle*) A new pastor attracts more then pious admiration among his congregation.

Terence Faherty (*God's Instrument*) Ten years after a devastating train wreck, a newspaper reporter discovers the truth behind a "miracle" phone call.

Mary Monica Pulver (*Father Hugh and the Kettle of St. Frideswide*) Egged on by an officious abbess, a clumsy monk uses the miracle of faith to discover a chicken thief at the Royal Abbey.

Ralph McInerny (*The Dunne Deal*) Soon after a pearl necklace, a Kruggerand, and one a hundred thousand lire note turn up in a church poor box, these same items are listed as stolen. What is the motive for this pilfered donation?

Carolyn Wheat (*Remembered Zion*) The distressing memory of a Kristallnacht accentuates the horror of religious strife in Europe.

Serita Stevens (*In a Jewish Vein*) A trip to Romania to carry out an adoption brings three Americans into a strange world where a hospitable vampire brings them closer to the Messiah.

New
from
Intrigue Press

WORLDKRIME

Bringing you the best crime fiction from
around the world.

Starting November 2001

CYPRUS

The Viper's Kiss *by Paris Aristides*

Middle-aged private eye Chrisostomos Zaras leaves his native Athens to find a lost fortune on the ethnically torn island of Cyprus. With the help of his taxi-driver sidekick, Zaras uncovers a plot involving Greek mobsters, drug trafficking, corrupt officials, and murderous Turks, with hidden agendas around every corner.

STOCKHOLM

The Last Draw *by Elisabet Peterzen*

Husband-and-wife journalist team, Erik and Katrin Skafte, are in hot pursuit of killer who is systematically murdering a string of victims in the Stockholm area. The victims seem completely unrelated but for one fact: they are all men. With the police coming up empty-handed, Erik and Katrin conduct their own investigation hoping for a publishing scoop. The pieces slowly drop into place, until a surprise twist leads to an unsettling conclusion.

BARCELONA

Study in Lilac *by Maria-Antònia Oliver*

Lònia has two problems on her hands: Sebastiana, a pregnant young rape victim whom Lònia has taken in off the streets; and Ms. Gaudí, a mysterious antique dealer who is trying to locate three men she claims defrauded her. Lònia's search for the three men takes her from private, opulent estates to the seedy docks of Barcelona, and a shocking discovery that will test the strength of her moral convictions. A fast-paced, fast-talking thriller that raises important social issues.

SYDNEY

Scream Black Murder
by Philip McLaren

New Year's Day. The bodies of a young Aboriginal
woman and her boyfriend are discovered in Redfern,
brutally murdered. Koori detectives Gary Leslie and Lisa Fuller, from the
new Aboriginal Homicide Unit of the NSWPD, are assigned to their first
case. Then a young white woman is killed and the pressure on the young
detectives to find the killer—fuelled by an increasingly frenzied media—
becomes unbearable….

FRANCE

Detective Lauriant Investigates *by Grant Wood*

Two deftly crafted mysteries set in 1960's France, starring the cynical, yet
compassionate Superintendent Lauriant. Having been banished to the
province of Vendee, Lauriant quickly finds himself back at work as the sui-
cide of a Count leaves many unanswered questions, and the dead man's
son as the chief suspect. In the second novella, a suspicious antique dealer
is found dead in a ditch, and the Superintendent's investigation draws him
into a provincial world of deadly entangled relationships.

AMSTERDAM

Murder in Amsterdam *by Baantjer*

In this hardcover English edition of the first two novellas by the Dutch
master, Inspector DeKok delves into Amsterdam's famed red-light district
following the murder of a much loved prostitute. In the second story,
DeKok must come to terms with an ethical quandary of whether to commit burglary and tamper with evidence to trap the murderer of young
women before he kills again. Baantjer has been hailed as the Dutch Sir
Arthur Conan Doyle for his knowledge of esoterica and three dimensional
characterizations.

INTRIGUE'S EXPANDING STABLE OF AUTHORS (AND THEIR SLEUTHS AND SETTINGS) INCLUDES:

Connie Shelton: The Charlie Parker Series (New Mexico)
"Charlie is slick, appealing and nobody's fool—just what readers want in an amateur sleuth." — Booklist

Sophie Dunbar: The Eclaire Series (New Orleans)
". . . an energetic, sensuous romp that is particularly refreshing. Mysteries don't get more fun than this." — LA Times

Steve Brewer: (New Mexico)
The Bubba Mabry, P.I. Series
"Brewer seems incapable of writing a boring paragraph." — Albuquerque Journal
The Drew Gavin Series
"A well-written, stylish noir caper." — Booklist

Alex Matthews: The Cassidy McCabe Series (Chicago)
"In McCabe [Matthews] depicts a spunky woman, divorced, unsure of romance, vulnerable yet self-sufficient. A frisky brew to be sure." — Chicago Sun-Times

George Grayson: The Jason Behr Series (Philadelphia)
". . . bite-your-nails suspense, [A] remarkably adept thriller." — Publishers Weekly

Aileen Schumacher: The Tory Travers Series (Florida/New Mexico)
". . . cliffhanger plot, mordant wit, and memorable characters." — Library Journal

M.K. Preston: The Chantalene Series (Oklahoma)
". . . an unusual heroine, idiosyncratic characters, a bucolic setting, and an intriguing plot. Strongly recommended." — Library Journal

Susan Slater: The Ben Pecos Series (New Mexico)
" . . . effectively combines an appealing mix of new and existing characters and beautiful, even mystical, descriptions of northern New Mexico." — Booklist